Bono's Hope
Forever Midnight MC
Book Three

Victoria Gale

Published in 2020 by

Deryn Publishing

United Kingdom

Second Edition

© 2020 Deryn Publishing

All characters, places and events are fictional. Any resemblance to real persons, places or events is purely coincidental.

The moral rights of the author have been asserted.

All rights reserved. No part of this publication may be reproduced, copied, stored or distributed in any form, without prior written permission of the publisher

"The strength of a family, like the strength of an army, is in its loyalty to each other."

– Mario Puzo

PROLOGUE

Hope

"Hey, don't work too late," Sarah said as she powered down her computer and stood, grabbing her bag. "You'll make us all look bad."

I smiled and picked up the files from my desk to wave at her. "You have no worries there. As soon as I've finished logging these, I'm outta here." Damn right, I was. Bono had taken the afternoon off work to have his tattoo finished, and I was itching to see the results. Besides, I had one week left working at Ashley Park Accountancy before I started college full-time. I liked my boss, but I wasn't about to do more work than I had to. If these numbers didn't need to be ready for first thing in the morning, I wouldn't be staying now.

Sarah laughed and waved goodbye, and I settled down to stare at the numbers on the papers in front of me and the spreadsheet on my monitor. I might as well have been banging my head against the wall for all the good it was doing. Whenever

I tried to focus and finish the work, I found my mind drifting to Bono and how he'd looked when I saw him this morning. He wore a simple, skin-tight black T-shirt that clung to his body like a second skin, highlighting every bulge in his chest and arms. What I'd give to trace those muscles with my tongue right now.

I cleared my throat and shifted in my seat, trying to ignore the wetness flooding my panties before casting a glance around the office. Empty. Thank fuck. I might be leaving, but I didn't need a thousand questions on why I couldn't get the big cheesy grin from my face. Just thinking of the reason for that grin had my core throbbing all over again.

I slapped the palm of my hand against my forehead and told myself to focus. The sooner I was finished here, the sooner I could get home to that hulk of a man and do whatever the hell I wanted with him. And I wanted to do a lot.

"You're still here," Kate Ashley, my boss, said, making me jump up from my seat and bang my knee against the desk. "Sorry, I didn't mean to scare you."

"You didn't... I mean, you surprised me. I didn't realize anyone was still here."

"Neither did I." Kate glanced around the empty office and turned off a few of the strip lights that illuminated vacant desks. "It looks like we're the last ones. Are you planning on staying all night?"

I laughed. "Not at all. I just have to finish typing up the Daniels figures, and then I'm off. I shouldn't be more than half an hour, tops."

"I shouldn't be much longer myself. Are you headed out the front door?" I nodded in response. "In that case, I'll close up the back when I go out, and you remember to lock up the front, okay?"

"Will do."

"Great." She looked at the remaining lights. "Don't forget to switch everything off when you leave," she said.

"Not a problem. Have a great night, Kate."

"You too, Hope. I'll see you in the morning."

Kate left, and I lifted the papers from my desk to bury my face in them for a few seconds while berating myself.

"Right." I placed them firmly on the desk, took a deep breath, and sat up straight. "Let's get this done."

Ten minutes later, and I had made some progress, but my mind couldn't focus on anything other than Bono. I looked at the ring on my finger. A stunning white gold solitaire twist diamond ring. 18ct. It cost more than Bono should have spent, but he said I was worth it.

Maybe the reason I couldn't focus was that I knew just how lucky I was to have met him. We'd both grown up in the system and bounced from foster home to foster home. But fate brought us together at fifteen when we landed in the same home together. Now we had an apartment of our own, and Bono had a good job and wanted to support me through college. Life just couldn't get any better than this. It was more than I ever thought possible, growing up the way I did.

Bono was perfection in a muscle wrapped bundle of deliciousness, and he was all mine. As soon as I got home, I would push him up against the wall and demand that he fuck me.

A door clicked shut down the hall, and more lights went off. I sighed. Great! Now I was the only one stuck working late.

"Finish this, and you can go home," I reminded myself.

A few minutes later, a soft knock came from the front door. When it opened, my heart jumped into my throat, and I realized that I hadn't shut it. A million thoughts swam through my mind. Another benefit of growing up in the system: I knew how to fight. I also knew it was better to hide and get the hell out of there instead of trying. I debated the possibility of running out the back but knew Kate would have locked up and I wouldn't be able to get out. A better option would be hiding under my desk, but better still would be hiding in the stationery closet only a few feet away. I stood, but my feet froze, and my worry turned to relief when Bono called my name.

"Hope," he called a second time.

"At my desk," I said. "What are you doing here?"

Bono emerged through the door by the reception area, and crossed the office, moving toward me with a sexy smile on his face. My first instinct was to rush towards him. And I was never inclined to fight my first instincts. I ran as if I hadn't seen him in a year and flung myself into his arms. My heart raced, and every part of me wanted to kiss and devour him. To feel the power of those strong, tight muscles against my body. I claimed his lips so thoroughly, I left no doubt in his mind that he was mine. Always mine.

I clung to his muscular shoulders and continued that kiss until my core throbbed with need, and I feared my legs would fall from beneath me.

"I missed you too," Bono said when we finally pulled apart.

"What are you doing here?"

"I noticed your car outside when I passed and wanted to check in and see why you were still working."

I growled and rested my head against his chest before glancing back at my desk. "I have some paperwork to finish up," I said.

Bono took my hand and walked me back to my desk. "Anything I can help with?" he asked.

"No. It's not difficult. Just mind-numbing, and I'm having trouble focusing..." I bit my lip and turned to face him.

"Actually," I said, stepping closer. "There is something you can do to help."

My heart pounded, and my core throbbed. I glanced around the empty office. Fuck it, I thought. Instead of letting go of Bono's hand, I held tighter and walked backward, pulling him toward the stationery closet a few feet to the left of my desk. I opened the door all the way and backed in, flicking on the light. Bono raised an eyebrow. He knew what I wanted. He stepped through the door and kicked it shut.

"Are you sure?" he asked, though a cheeky grin played at the edge of his lips. "This is your place of work."

Fuck, yes!

"Soon to be my ex-place-of-work," I answered, my eyes focused on his. "No one else is here." I pulled his leather jacket off and tossed it to the ground. I noted the bandage on the top of his arm, covering his completed tattoo, but resisted pulling it off to look. There would be plenty of time for that later.

Bono pushed his body tight against mine. His tongue probed my mouth. I backed up further. Heat filled my entire body, and my core tingled. I wanted him so badly, I thought I'd burst before he had the chance to touch me.

I reached beneath my skirt and removed my panties. Within seconds, my hands were on his belt buckle and I was licking my lips in anticipation of freeing his bulging cock.

"We have to be quick," I whispered and nibbled his earlobe.

He laughed. "Then you'd better come quick." His breath was like molten fire against my neck. His teeth scraped along my throat. He pushed my shirt to the side, and they continued to the hollow of my shoulder.

"Not a problem," I said, breathless.

My fingers fumbled to undo the last fastening on his jeans. His cock sprung free, huge and as hard as a rock. Without hesitating, Bono pushed his hand between my legs and brushed his fingers up my thigh, before stroking them along my wet folds.

"You're all ready for me," he said.

"I've been waiting for this all day," I answered.

"A gentleman should never keep a lady waiting."

My heart sped up as he pulled me down to the floor on top of him. He gripped my hips and lifted me in place with the head of his cock at my entrance. He pulled down roughly and I cried out as he filled me with one stroke. Even though I was on top, Bono used the muscles in his strong arms and guided the actions, owning me, and taking me hard and deep.

Blackness filled my vision as my orgasm hit. I cried out. Sheer bliss rocked through me. My core tightened around his cock, milking out his climax as he came alongside me.

"Oh fuck," Bono said. "You are fucking incredible."

"Oh, fuck is exactly right," I answered. Delirious with pleasure, I wilted against his chest.

After a moment, I chuckled softly. "This was supposed to get you out of my system so I could finish work," I said.

Bono put on a mock sad face. "You wanted me out of your system?"

"Only for half an hour or so." I stood and found my panties, sliding them on. They would be sopping, but I could deal with that at home. I sighed with a slight pang of regret as Bono fastened his jeans and his cock disappeared. "You'd better go, or I'll be here all night."

"Are you sure there's nothing I can help you with?"

I smiled and brushed my lips against his before sighing again. "There's plenty you can help me with as soon as we're back home," I said.

Bono rested his forehead against mine. "I'm yours to command."

"Actually, tonight, I think I might be yours."

Bono grabbed my bottom and squeezed, pulling me in tighter to him so that I could feel his cock hardening again.

I slapped him on his bottom. "Home," I commanded. "And grab a pizza for us to share later."

"I thought I was the one who was going to do the commanding," he said.

"You will."

Bono laughed and we left the stationery closet. He lingered for a while, reluctant to leave me alone, but I insisted, and he eventually agreed to go.

"Ham, mushroom, and pineapple," I called after him.

He turned and scrunched his face at me. Having pineapple on a pizza was a long-running topic for debate the world over and our household was no different. "It's like a party in my mouth," I called before he ducked through the door.

"I'll show you a party in your mouth," he countered.

"Command and it shall be done."

"Then I command, ham, mushrooms, and no pineapple."

"Just go," I said before adding that we could settle for pineapple on just half.

I went back to work with a smile on my face, for much the same reason it was earlier. But, at least, I had been sated for twenty minutes or so, and I could finally focus and finish.

Not five minutes later, the faint squeak of the back door, barely audible above my breathing, sounded in my ears. I held my breath.

Fuck!

I hadn't heard it earlier. I'd only noted Kate's office door. I glanced overhead. When I thought she'd left, Kate must have just been switching off the lights in the corridor.

Fuck! I thought again.

If she heard me and Bono… Then what? She'd fire me? I shook my head. Probably not. But still… how could I face her in the morning?

I took deep breaths and tried to steady my pulse. What's done is done. If Kate hadn't felt the need to mention anything tonight when we were alone, it was doubtful she would say anything tomorrow. Maybe, I'd get a little talk about my conduct on my last day.

Only when footsteps sounded in the corridor and I heard another door did I question whether it was Kate at all. They seemed to be coming nearer, not moving farther away. And if it was the back door I heard, wouldn't that have been Kate finally leaving?

I'd left the front door unlocked, and that now had me wondering if that meant the back door was in a similar state.

I tried not to worry, told myself it was nothing, but the unease flowing through my veins and making my skin crawl told me otherwise.

Not wanting to risk a beep when shutting down my computer, I switched off my monitor to remove its light. I grabbed my phone and pushed my bag way under my desk out of sight. The footsteps had stopped. I glanced at the stationery closet door.

A nagging voice inside my head told me I was being stupid, but my palms grew slick.

I punched 911 into my smartphone and hovered my finger over the dial button. But hesitated in pushing it.

I rubbed my forehead. *This is so stupid.* I took a deep breath and decided the best thing to do was sneak to the corridor and take a look.

I inched forward, keeping my finger over the dial button. As I passed the last desk, nearest the door, I grabbed a pair of scissors and held them ready as a weapon.

The door to the corridor was wide open. I stood against the wall to the side for a second, steadying my nerves. Then peeked around. I let out a huff of relief when, through the window in her door, I saw Kate sitting at her desk, typing away with headphones on. I was about to step into the corridor when someone shifted in another office five doors down. I jerked back out of view, being as quiet as possible. The faint squeak of the door opposite the one where I'd noted movement greeted me, and I wondered if whoever was there was giving the rooms a sweep to make sure they were empty before moving on. If we were lucky, maybe they'd take the equipment from those rooms and not see a need to move further into the building. Though I doubted that would be the case.

Kate. Oh shit. I had to alert her.

I decided to try and draw whoever it was into the main office. Maybe, if I hid and they came in here, I could quickly dive through to Kate and we could get out of the building while calling for help.

I glanced at the 911 undialed on my phone and switched to text messaging before quickly firing off a distress message to the police.

I then moved and hid under the desk I'd taken the scissors from. Doing a mental run-through of the room, I placed Stuart's desk as the furthest away from where I hid. Drawing the intruder there would give me the best option for getting through to Kate.

I dialed Stuart's number, and even though I knew it was coming, jumped when the phone rang, filling the otherwise silent office with noise.

I stared at the door, held my breath, and willed the intruder to take the bait and walk through to investigate.

Kate's shocked scream and the gunshot that followed greeted me instead.

Without thinking, I rushed from under the desk toward Kate's office, but froze in the corridor doorway when through her window, I saw a man walk to her side of the desk and point a gun down at the floor. Kate was nowhere to be seen. I knew she had to be lying on the floor, and that there was nothing I could do for her.

With tears in my eyes, and sobbing gasps rising in my throat, I lifted my smartphone, turned the video on, and zoomed in to film inside Kate's office. Just in time to see the man fire two shots at the ground. I tried not to cry out, to fall to the floor in shock. Instead, I darted back into the office and retook my hiding place under the desk.

When the man appeared in the doorway, I held my one hand tight over my mouth and prayed he couldn't hear the beating of my heart, but kept the smartphone in my other trained on the door, even while I knew that if he caught me, it would be for nothing.

When he turned and left, and I heard the back door close moments later, I remained where I was, too afraid to move. But the idea that I could still do something to help Kate eventually drove me out. I glanced at my phone and realized I was still filming. Only three minutes and twenty-three seconds had passed since I'd first started recording, but it felt like a lifetime. I kept filming and edged cautiously to Kate's office on legs that barely supported me.

My pulse raced and my stomach wanted to turn itself inside out. I entered Kate's office and moved behind her desk. I dropped my phone and fell to my knees at the sight that greeted me.

Kate's lifeless body was crumpled in a heap on the cold gray carpeted floor of her office. Blood pooled around her head and covered her chest.

"I'm so sorry," I whispered.

I just sat there staring. Afraid to move. Afraid to breathe.

Only when I gasped did I notice the smell of smoke in the air. I didn't want to leave Kate, but the building filled with smoke so quickly, I had no choice. I grabbed my phone and darted out the front door, dialing the police as I did so, even though the sound of sirens could be heard in the distance.

CHAPTER ONE

(Ten Years Later)

Hope

"Not gonna happen," I said, knowing that I sounded like a petulant child. "There is absolutely no way on Earth I would ever let you set me up on another blind date. Not again."

"Not gonna happen," I said, knowing that I sounded like a petulant child. "There is absolutely no way on Earth I would ever let you set me up on another blind date. Not again."

"Apart from the fact you're lonely and need somebody in your life." Danielle was meant to be my best friend. She knew where I stood on dates and on men. It frustrated the hell out of me that every few months she got it into her mind that I needed someone.

I rubbed at the ache forming in my head and glared at her.

"Look," she said. "I know the last two blind dates weren't exactly stellar—" she matched my glare with one of her own "—

but I think that's more down to you than the men I set you up with."

"Yeah, right," I said.

"Do you really want to spend the rest of your life alone?" Danielle asked, ignoring the sarcasm in my voice. "Come on, Hope, seriously. What have you got to lose?"

I looked at the bagel in front of me and pushed it away, my appetite lost. The sounds in the coffee shop drilled into my brain and amplified my headache. I shut Danielle's voice out as she droned on and on about how happy she was with Charles, and how I needed to find someone the way she had, someone I could grow old with.

But that was the point, even though I could never tell her. I had someone I wanted to grow old with. But that was over. I sighed, remembering that fateful day a decade ago.

God! Had it really been so long?

A faint smile played at the edge of my lips as I remembered that last time with Bono in the stationery closet. If only I'd left when he did. I could have gone into the office early the next morning to finish the work needed. I could have done a million things differently, and I'd thought about each and every one of them countless times over the years.

Danielle was right. There was nothing wrong with the men she set me up with. It was all me. How could I hope to have a relationship with anyone when I'd forever be in love with Bono? Even if I did find someone new, there was no saying I wouldn't have to up sticks and move on again. Special Agent Weathers from WITSEC could be knocking down my door and have me moving to a new state with a new identity any day or night.

No. Better to keep myself to myself and accept that as my fate.

"Jesus, Hope," Danielle said. "Don't you want to be happy?"

"No. That ship has sailed," I said after a moment. "Besides, I'm busy."

Danielle rolled her eyes and took a sip of her coffee. "You are not too busy. We work in the same office, remember? When you're not with me, you go straight home and don't say a word to anyone, and don't you pretend otherwise."

"That is so not true. You know I go to the range on weekends, and there's my Jiu-jitsu class every Tuesday and Friday."

"Yay, you like to go out and kick or shoot things."

I couldn't help but smile at the expression on her face but sighed when I remembered the reason why I did those things.

Danielle reached across the table and squeezed my hand. "I'm not asking you to jump in and marry the guy after the first date. I'm just asking that you meet with him and see if you hit it off. If nothing else, you'll get a free dinner out of it. You need someone, Hope. I know how lonely and closed off you are, even if you've never shared what made you that way."

I found it a little unnerving that Danielle could read me like a book, and worried that we were getting too close. It was getting hard to keep things from her.

I took a deep, calming breath, slowly released it, and hailed the waiter for the bill.

Maybe I was the one who needed to call my handler and tell him it was time to move on.

I slumped back in my chair and felt all the resolve go out of me. One meeting. Just to keep Danielle happy, and then I'd have to seriously think about a change of scenery.

"He gets one date," I said. "And it has to be somewhere crowded with lots of people." Somewhere he wouldn't make a scene if I decided the date was more trouble than it was worth. Which I already knew it was.

"One date," Danielle agreed. "For now. You won't regret it."

~

You won't regret it, I scoffed to myself, four hours later when I handed my car keys over to the valet. I already did. My stomach knotted and my heart pounded so hard in my chest, I thought even the doorman could hear it.

Despite the rush to get ready and my nerves at meeting Jim — Fuck! Was his name Jim or Tim? — I'd pulled out all the stops. At least then, Danielle couldn't say I didn't try. My body was freshly shaven and smelt delicious, even if I did say so myself, like cherry-blossom body wash. My long brown hair was styled so curls tousled gently over one shoulder, and my lips were coated with pure-passion pink lipstick. Even my dress was chosen to accentuate my best features. It was a gold, lace bodycon dress that clung to me in all the right places and made me feel like a million dollars. My only regret was that Bono wasn't the one who got to see me in it.

I huffed out a sigh. Ten years! Jesus. I needed to stop living in the past.

I nodded my thanks to the doorman as he ushered me inside and couldn't help but notice his eyes traveling the length of my body. Yep, I looked good.

Maybe it was time I gave someone a shot. Jim… or Tim, this just might be your lucky night. Depending on how you look at things.

With my head held high and a new resolve keeping my back straight, I walked towards the hostess.

The restaurant was filled with people. Their voices created a vibe that buzzed through my skin and caused me to shiver. I'd never eaten at The Chandlery before. It was way too expensive for my pocket. Plus, I heard you had to reserve a table two months in advance. Danielle's set-up either had to be well connected or pretty rich to pull tonight off.

The churning in my stomach increased as I scanned the faces around the bar, wondering if my date was amongst them.

A large man, more muscular and broader than any of the others, stood and smiled at me, but it was the man a few seats away from him that caught my eye. He wore a suit, which even from the back, I could tell was designer-labeled. His hair was short and dark, and I could see the briefest outline of his face.

The heady scent of wine dizzied my senses and made me realize how parched my throat had become. I stared at the man as dread built inside me, even as the muscle-man made his way towards me. My stomach churned and I thought I might throw up.

"You must be Hope," the muscle-man said. "Is everything okay?" I didn't answer, couldn't answer. Muscle-man, whose name may be Jim or Tim, I no longer cared, followed my gaze. "Do you know him?" he asked.

The man at the bar turned fully to face me and my heart sank. He lifted his glass and raised it as though in a toast before taking a sip. His eyes were dark, cold, and calculating. Any doubts I might have had fled me as he stared me down.

"I'm sorry," I said to Muscle-man, not turning to look at him. "This was a mistake. I have to go." Without another word, I backpedaled out the door, too afraid to take my eyes off the man at the bar. Mickey Dolmilo. The man who, ten years ago, I saw murder Kate Ashley.

Even as the doorman asked me if everything was okay, I backed away from the building. Anxiety pumped through my veins as I glanced up and down the street. Despite the late hour, we were in one of the busiest parts of town, full of bars and restaurants. He wouldn't try anything here, not with all these people around. Would he?

I was used to scanning my surroundings and watching my back, but after all this time, I'd held out a faint shred of hope that this day would never come. I never truly believed it would. Even as I'd testified against him and the Marshals warned me how dangerous he was — as if I needed telling — I still held onto the hope that things could go back to normal, that I could have a life. I swallowed down a lump forming in my throat and wondered how he could have found me.

The valet asked me for my ticket, but I shook my head. That's what Dolmilo wanted, for me to get in my car, to run, and be alone. I had to do something. So far, he hadn't moved, but through the glass door, I noted muscle-man kept looking at him as though he wanted to challenge him.

Damn it! Typical of my luck that Danielle finally found someone I might have hit it off with. Though maybe it was his good fortune that we hadn't met sooner, and he'd become more embroiled in my dangerous life.

After a moment of indecision, I slowly removed my heels and bolted down the street with them in my hands. Maybe in the crowds, I'd be able to duck into another bar or restaurant without being seen.

A million thoughts ran through my head. I could approach security at one of the bars, although that might mean risking their life too. I should call the police, but a nagging voice inside told me that was a mistake. The best they could do is call the Marshals and have me moved somewhere new. But the thought that the Marshals were the only people who knew where to find me and had to have told Dolmilo flashed foremost in my mind.

A man stepped out of an alleyway in front of me. I skidded to a halt to avoid hitting him, but wasn't fast enough to prevent him from reaching out and grabbing my wrist.

"Hey, slow down," he said.

I reacted without thinking and did the easiest thing I knew how. Gripping my shoes tight, I kept my elbow low, found a strong, squatting stance, and bent my elbow towards him until he had no choice but to let go of my wrist. By now, a few guys across the street had noticed what was happening and were making their way towards us. I could tell from the look on the face of the man I ran into that he debated grabbing me again, but obviously decided against it.

I didn't waste the opportunity I'd been given and ran.

"I'm fine," I called behind me, hoping that the men would disperse, and nobody would get into trouble.

I ducked into a bar that I knew had three other entrances, left through one of them, and weaved my way through four more before finding a corner in a noisy club where I could barely think. I choked back sobs, ran my fingers over my head, and held my breath, wondering if my heart would explode and what the hell I was going to do. I waited for almost an hour, but decided I had to leave before the streets got too quiet and I'd be easy to spot.

A group of young women was sitting at a booth on the other side of the room. They had a pile of jackets next to them. Searching in my purse, I pulled a hair-tie out and quickly braided my hair and tied it back out of the way. Then I counted the cash I had. A little over four-hundred dollars. Having to constantly look over my shoulder also meant that I always carried a fair amount of cash. I pulled out five twenties and put the rest away before walking over to the girls.

"Hi," I said, having to shout over the music. "I hate to ask this, but I wonder if any of you would be willing to part with a jacket? I have a hundred dollars I can pay you."

"Girl. If you need my jacket, you do not need to pay for it." The young woman closest to me delved into the pile and pulled out what I assumed must be her coat. It looked like it was worth way more than the hundred dollars I'd offered.

"No really, I couldn't."

"Do you think we haven't noticed you sitting in the corner all alone? From the look on your face, you're avoiding a bad ex or something. I've been there, trust me, and if the least I can do is give you my jacket, then that's what I'm gonna do."

She thrust the jacket at me, and I took it, not bothering to correct her assumption I was hiding from an ex.

"Thank you," I said and slipped it on. "Is there any way I can return it to you?"

"If you get the chance, just drop it over the bar. Tell them it's for Trish. My brother's the owner."

"Thank you, Trish," I said and gave her a warm smile before nodding and bidding goodbye to her and the girls she was with.

I pushed through the crowds but hesitated by the side of the door. My stomach roiled. I couldn't see outside. I'd settled in this club purely because of the lack of windows and the ability to see inside, but that also meant I couldn't see outside. The streets could already be quiet. I could open the door and walk straight into Dolmilo. I could walk outside and get a bullet to the head.

A hand landed on my shoulder, and I jumped before turning ready to strike out. I stopped my fist a fraction of a second before it slammed into Trish's face.

"I'm so sorry," I said.

"Girl, you are jumpier than a frog on a pogo stick." She pointed towards the back of the room, beyond the dance floor. "My car is parked right outside the rear exit. I'll take you wherever you need to go."

"I couldn't ask you to do that. It wouldn't be safe for you with me."

"You didn't ask. I offered. I can go out, make sure no one's around, get the car started and the door open ready for you to dive in. You can come out in a crowd with a few friends of mine. As soon as you're in the car, you can duck down so as not to be seen."

I debated her offer, wanting for all the world to say no. She'd already done too much for me, but what other choice did I have?

"We won't proceed if you see anyone watching," I said when Trish echoed my own thoughts.

"We can wait in this club all night if necessary. We'll get you out and somewhere safe without anyone seeing."

Somewhere safe. That would be nice. I just wished I knew exactly where that was.

CHAPTER TWO

Bono

Midnight Anchor was full of a contingency of brothers tonight. Not unusual for a bar owned by Forever Midnight MC, but what was unusual was the lack of any other patrons and the presence of dolly girls. Cherrie and Greg ran the place, and they had strict rules about allowing the women who allowed brothers to fuck them for entertainment as though they were blow-up dolls through the door. Those women were normally reserved for the clubhouse. But tonight was a special occasion and they understood that some of the brothers liked to celebrate in different ways from others. Dolly girls were groupies for bikers, and like any club, Forever Midnight had a gang of them who liked to hang around at the clubhouse and see who was willing to accommodate their needs. They were all too happy to spread their legs and allow a brother to pin them down and fuck them, no matter who was watching.

That fact had always disturbed me. It was as though the

women had no self-respect. That didn't mean I hadn't partaken when the need arose. I wasn't a monk. For years fucking or more alcohol than was good for me had been the only things that ensured me a good night's sleep.

I'd question why my appetites had changed in the last year or so, and the idea of fucking a dolly girl had moved from a faint dislike to one of outright repulsion, but the answer was as easy to spot as the massive fucker grinning from ear to ear beside me.

"I can't believe I'm a dad," Cane said, shaking his head as he took a swig of his beer.

Caleb clapped him on the back. "You and me both."

"How the fuck did this happen?"

Lucky laughed. "If no one's given you *'the talk'* by now, I sure as fuck can't help you."

Everyone laughed, and Cane clipped Lucky over the head, but the stupid grin never left his face. He sighed, shook his head, and took another sip of beer.

I was happy for my brother. He was a good man, and he deserved a good woman like Thea. The fact that they'd welcomed their first baby into the world this morning and had asked me to be godfather along with Cane's blood-brother, Caleb, made me happy beyond belief. But seeing what Cane had with Thea, and what Caleb had found with Amber, had pushed my past front and center in my mind. Not a day went by when I didn't think of Hope and the life denied us, but, I guess, it was just fucking easier to live with when those closest to me were also alone.

Fuck! How fucking selfish did that sound?

I finished my beer and slammed the bottle down on the bar. "A round of tequila," I called to Greg. He grabbed seven shot glasses and poured us each a drink, before setting the bottle on the counter next to them and lifting one of the glasses and raising it in the air.

"To Cane, Thea, and their beautiful baby girl," he said before swigging back the fiery liquid.

We each joined him in the toast, while Cane raised his glass just to Thea and the baby. "A girl," he said. "What the fuck do I know about being the father of a little girl?"

Caleb laughed again and shook his head. "Don't ask me. I'm just getting used to it myself."

The others returned to their beers while I grabbed the bottle of tequila under the watchful eye of Greg. We had an understanding. He was to stop me whenever I looked on the verge of drinking too much, but I wasn't in the mood to let him stop me tonight. Maybe, he sensed that, as he huffed out a breath and turned his attention to serving someone else.

I took a swig from the bottle and noticed a curvy redhead watching me from beneath her eyelashes. Rosie. There was a time or two I would have rushed her upstairs and had her on her knees in front of me. Those days had passed, even if she had been trying to rekindle them of late.

She patted the stool next to her, but I shook my head. She pouted and turned her attention to another brother across the room. One dick's as good as another.

I took another swig from the bottle, feeling bad that my mood wasn't a match for the celebration at hand.

Cane nudged me with his elbow. "You alright?" he asked. I nodded. "I noticed Rosie calling you over. You can leave if you need a fuck."

"Rosie's not what I need," I said.

Cane nodded at my bottle. "And that is?"

I lifted it and looked at the swirling golden contents. "No," I said, huffing out a breath. "This isn't what I need either." I put the bottle back on the bar and rubbed my hand over my face. "I'm fucking sorry," I said. "I am so fucking happy for you. I really am. I just…"

"I know, Bono. I know." Cane put his arm around me. He was the only brother who really did know. The only one I'd told about Hope and how I'd lost her. The only one who knew of the many more people I'd lost after that in Afghanistan.

"All right," Caleb said, clapping his hands together. "The night is fucking young. And it'll be the last one Cane sees in a while. Who wants to take our group to the back room and get wasted in peace?"

"I sure as hell do," I said and asked Greg for another round of beers to carry through with us.

I shook all thoughts from my head and vowed to have a good time. This evening was about Cane and his new family, not me.

The beers came fast and frequent, but it was mostly the others who drank them. Rex and Lucky cracked jokes for a while, but soon returned to the main bar to mingle and find women. Only Cane, Caleb, Jameson, and I remained in the back room when my mobile vibrated in my pocket.

I pulled it out and stared at the screen. The number wasn't one I recognized, and the display recorded it as being registered in Arizona.

"Hello," I said, answering the call. A gasping sob greeted me. "Who is this?" I asked.

"Bono."

"Who's asking?"

"Bono Travers? It is you, isn't it? After all this time, you have the same number."

I wanted to be angry, but the female voice on the other end sounded faintly familiar and was obviously distressed. "Who is this?" I asked again.

A breath huffed along the line. "It's Hope."

A ball of fire grew in my belly as hot as the flames that took Hope's body from me. I stood from the table, vaguely aware that the room had fallen silent. My fists clenched around my phone and spittle flew from my mouth as I spoke into it.

"I will fucking kill you," I said, not knowing who this could be or what game they were playing.

"Bono. It's… it's really me." The words were choked out between sobs, her breath ragged. "You have to believe me."

Despite my anger, I listened closely to the voice, wondering if I'd recognize it as someone from my past, someone who wanted to hurt me. The voice had matured but something inside made me believe it was Hope's. But that was nothing more than a fucking foolish fantasy. "Hope's dead," I said. "I buried her myself."

Cane turned to Jameson. "Get Rex," he said before nodding to me.

I knew what he wanted. The brothers had turned the far end of the room into a makeshift office about a year back when Greg was in the hospital and we were reluctant to leave Cherrie at the bar on her own. Next to a laptop and a landline on the desk lining the wall, Cherrie had placed a pot of pens and a notepad. Cane ripped off a sheet from the pad and handed it to me along with a pen. I switched the call to hands free and placed the phone on the center table so everyone could hear.

"It's really me, Bono. The US Marshals only made it look like I'd died in the fire."

"And why the fuck would they do that?" I asked at the same time as jotting down the caller's number.

I swallowed the anger bubbling up from inside and tried to keep my senses, despite the confusion swirling through my head.

I'd never forget the night two police officers knocked on my door and told me Hope had died, killed in a fire set to cover the murder of her boss, Kate Ashley. I wanted the fucker responsible dead. They wouldn't let me near the case, and the reporting was kept to a minimum as it turned out he was some big shot mafia hitman. I couldn't even learn what crimes he'd been charged with. But an officer called to let me know he'd been convicted. Life with no option of parole.

"I witnessed Kate's murder. They needed me to enter witness protection and testify."

I shook my head, wanting with all my heart to believe what I was hearing. "I fucking buried a body," I yelled into the phone as tears filled my eyes.

"It wasn't me," she sobbed as Rex and Jameson entered the room with Lucky behind them. "Witness Protection only made you think that it was."

Cane didn't hesitate in taking the paper from my hand and

giving it to Rex, who turned on the laptop.

"Remember that night," she continued. "You came to the office. We... we went into the stationery closet."

"How the fuck do you know that?" My words held venom, but hers had surprised me.

I turned to Cane, who raised an eyebrow. My stomach churned. It couldn't be Hope, could it?

"We were going to have pizza," she continued, her voice becoming soft and barely audible. "You didn't want pineapple."

I leaned on the table with my head low and my hands resting either side of the phone. "Who the fuck likes pineapple on their pizza?" I asked, my voice equally quiet.

"I do."

"It's like a party in the mouth," we both said at the same time.

"Hope."

"It's really me, Bono."

Rex stood from the laptop. "Just outside of Phoenix," he mouthed, having traced the number.

"Why now?" I asked. "After all this time." She was the love of my life. I'd never gotten over losing Hope. I had so many questions, not least of which was how she could leave me.

"I saw Mickey Dolmilo two nights ago. The guy who killed Kate. He stared right at me, and I ran. I haven't stopped running.

I… I just… You're the only person I trust."

"Impossible. Dolmilo got life."

The atmosphere in the room had been tense, but it suddenly felt as though the entire place had been filled with expanding foam, and all that cloying energy was pouring off Jameson in waves.

I stared at him as the person I was beginning to think of as Hope continued on the other end of the phone. "That's what I was told, too," she said. "But it was him, I'll never forget the look on his face."

"Where are you?" I asked, not taking my eyes off Jameson.

"No," Rex rushed towards me. "Don't answer that question," he screamed. "Not on this line. Call her back," he said and nudged his head at the phone by the laptop.

"You hear that?" I asked Hope. "I'm gonna end the call and phone back." Without waiting for a response, I ended the call while glaring at Rex.

"You have the same number you had ten years ago," he explained. "There's a reason you have to cut contact with everyone you know when you enter witness protection."

I nodded, understanding that my phone might be compromised. Though it was doubtful after all this time.

"What do you know about this Dolmilo?" Caleb asked Jameson, as I moved to the other phone.

"Nothing good," he answered. "I'll go and make some calls upstairs and see what I can find out." With that, he left the room. Caleb nodded to Lucky, who turned and followed after him.

"Bono," Hope said with evident relief in her voice when she answered the phone. "You called back."

"I said I would."

"Does that mean you believe me?"

"I don't know what to fucking believe," I answered. "Where are you? I'm coming to get you."

CHAPTER THREE

Bono

Thanks to Amber and her job at Denver International Airport, I'd been on the twenty-past-ten flight to Phoenix that night. The location Hope gave me matched the one Rex had traced, fueling my belief that she was who she said she was.

Two and a half hours later, I was driving the rental car Amber had also arranged toward the motel Hope was holed up in when my phone rang.

"Talk to me, Jameson?" I said, noting his name on the display before I answered.

"Mickey Dolmilo's out."

Fuck! "Do you think Hope's in serious trouble here?"

"She is. Dolmilo's a hired killer for various mob families. He's out on a technicality under appeal. That and all the evidence against him has conveniently been lost or destroyed."

"Wouldn't they have called Hope as a witness again?" I asked.

"You'd think."

I sighed and rubbed my hand over my face. "What's all this got to do with Hope?" I asked. Ten years was a long time to hold a grudge. "You think he's after revenge?"

"It's worse than that. Dolmilo needs to prove himself to get back in the business."

I turned off the main road and saw the motel in the distance. My heart raced. "Prove himself?"

"If he can't take care of his business and clean up his own mess, then why should anyone else trust him with theirs?"

Fuck! I thought again. "So, what you're telling me is that this fucker is a trained for-hire killer who needs to kill Hope to clear the way for him to get back in the game."

"I'm telling you, it's a miracle she's not already dead."

As if I didn't know that. I pulled the rental to a stop outside the motel. Despite being almost two in the morning, a few lights were on in some of the rooms, and the reception area was lit up like a Christmas tree. I glanced at the third floor where Hope had said she was. I'd told her to barricade the door and not move or make another phone call, unless she needed to call the police, until I got there. Her room was dark.

"Thanks, Jameson," I said.

He sighed down the phone. "Hurry home. We have a better chance of keeping her alive if we're all together and in familiar territory."

"I know." It was a thirteen-hour drive back to Castle Rock, but there weren't any non-stop flights out of Phoenix to Denver until 6:25 a.m., and that was full. I was beat, having been up for nineteen hours. But it wasn't the first time I'd needed to go without sleep for a few days, and it probably wouldn't be the last. I glanced back up at the room. "We'll be on the road within ten minutes," I said.

With a promise to try and get more information and possibly help from his contacts in New York, Jameson ended the call. I huffed out a breath and left the car.

No one challenged me when I bypassed the reception area and walked straight up to the third floor. I stood before the blue door of room thirty-seven for a second, my heart in my throat. I closed my eyes and tried to conjure Hope's face, her sparkling eyes and the dimples that formed in her cheeks when she smiled. It had grown harder over the years to pull her image to mind, but it was there in full glory tonight.

Fuck! If this wasn't her, I didn't know what I'd do.

While dread rolled in my stomach, I opened my eyes, took a deep breath, and knocked on the door. "Hope. It's me, Bono."

I heard movement on the other side of the door. The sound of shifting furniture. It stopped, and I stood frozen as though between one heartbeat and the next. The door opened a crack, and Hope's wide brown eyes greeted me.

Her face was the same, but older with a maturity I didn't remember. I shuddered. She was as beautiful as I remembered. My insides whirled in confusion, and I was bombarded with one emotion after another. Relief, love, anger, denial. But within it all, I felt strangely numb.

Hope looked at the ground and shifted from one foot to another. I hadn't known what to expect. During the flight, I'd pictured her running into my arms, me spinning her off her feet and kissing her the way she'd kissed me the last time we'd seen each other. Instead, neither of us moved.

"We should leave," I said, breaking the silence. "Grab your things."

"I'm wearing all that I have," she said, her voice barely above a whisper.

I took in the leggings and her oversized hooded-top and nodded before stepping back away from the door.

We walked to the reception, where I stood outside while Hope returned her key. We got in the car and on the road without saying a word to each other.

The drive would take forever with neither of us talking, but still, I couldn't bring myself to say anything. The road ahead lay empty and black, and a quietude filled the night. Only the turning of the tires and the faint whir of the engine broke the silence.

Hope twisted the ring on her finger, drawing my gaze. In the dark, it was hard to make out, but even though it was on the wrong hand, it looked like the one I'd given her all those years ago.

It had been a long time since I'd thought of the ring. Before I'd proposed, I'd teased her about her slender fingers and bet that she took a child's size just to get her ring size from her. I'd even managed to find out what sort of design she'd like by dragging her around jewelry shops under the pretense of wanting a new watch and commenting on a few rings while we were there. After that, and a lot of searching, I finally found the ring I thought perfect for her.

Unable to stop myself, I reached out and lifted her right hand to get a better look. I half expected her to flinch away from my touch, but she didn't.

"Is this...?" I asked. Hope nodded. "You kept it."

"I couldn't bring myself to part with it." I released her hand, but instead of pulling it back down to her lap, she stroked the bristles of my beard. "How long have you had this?" she asked.

I clasped onto her fingers to still them. "Not long," I answered, unsure why anger built inside me.

Hope must have sensed my mood. She pulled her hand away and shifted in her seat to stare out the window.

I studied the side of her face. A wariness reflected in eyes surrounded by dark circles. If that wasn't enough to show me the stress she'd been under, the furrow of her brow would.

For eight years, she'd been my whole life. From the time I first met her at fifteen until she died… until she left at twenty-three, she'd been my everything, and I'd never stopped loving her. Or rather, I now wondered, I never stopped loving the memory that used to be her. Otherwise, why would now be so difficult?

My chest clenched and I found it hard to breathe. Too many emotions warred inside me. I couldn't focus, couldn't think. For now, all I could do was stare at the road ahead and count down the hours until we reached Castle Rock.

"Did you marry someone else?" I found myself asking a while later.

"No. Did you?"

I shook my head. I wanted to tell her that there was never anyone but her for me, but the truth was, I didn't know who the hell she was. My Hope was there. I saw it in her every movement, in the way she held her head and crossed her legs even in the car, but ten years was a long time to be apart, and I'd changed so much. The me of ten years ago wouldn't recognize myself in the man I'd become. How much had Hope changed during that time as well?

"This was a mistake," Hope said, her eyes focused on the darkness outside. "You should drop me off—"

"The only mistake you made was running out on me ten years ago," I said, unable to stop the hurt and anger pouring out in my voice. I slammed my fists against the steering wheel. "What the fuck happened? Why the fuck didn't you come to me?"

"Dolmilo killed Kate," she said as she turned to face me, and I noted a tear streaming down her cheek, making me feel like the biggest fucking asshole in the world. "I was scared, confused. The police were there within seconds. They took my phone, didn't let me make a call. Before I knew what happened, I was in some orientation center in Washington, having counseling for the life I was being forced into. It just… it all happened so fast, and they said I had to cut all ties, that you thought I was dead, and it would be better for you if I stayed that way."

Her words made my anger shift from her to the fucking Marshals. They'd railroaded Hope into the program alone to suit their needs, never once thinking about what was best for her.

"I would have come with you," I said.

This time it was Hope's voice that filled with anger. "Don't you think I know that?" She wiped at the tears as though they were acid burning her cheeks. "Don't you think that not a day has gone by where I haven't questioned my every action? When

I've wanted to pick up the phone and call, even if that meant hanging up before speaking just to hear your voice?"

I shook my head. "You should have called me."

She shifted her gaze back out the window. "Yeah? Look how fucking well that's going for me now," she muttered, her voice full of derision.

Despite myself, a small smile crept onto my face. There was the Hope I knew. The one who'd sooner punch me in the fucking face than let me shout her down.

"All this time and you still haven't learned that pineapple has no place on a pizza," I said to try and break the tension.

"All this time, and you haven't learned that it does," she countered.

"Only for fucking crazy people."

Hope laughed. The same laugh I'd missed every day. When she sobered, she reached out and placed her hand on top of mine on the steering wheel. "I'm scared," she said. "This guy, this Dolmilo. I had the chance to learn all about him. He's not a good man. If he wants me dead, then I'm dead."

"Not gonna happen," I said, shaking my head. "Not again."

CHAPTER FOUR

Hope

I couldn't believe I was sitting in a car next to Bono with him driving along the road towards his home in Castle Rock. I couldn't believe he'd moved to Colorado when we'd grown up in L.A. We'd both spent a lifetime apart, and I couldn't imagine what he'd been through. There was a sadness in his eyes, and something told me it wasn't just my supposed death that had put it there.

I assessed his bearing. He was still all muscly perfection, but his muscles were a little leaner than they used to be, and his movements were more deliberate, as though he debated everything in his mind before acting on anything. He'd always been a little that way, but it was more obvious now.

After Trish had managed to successfully get me away from the club, I'd asked her to drive me to the bus station. When she realized I was running, she gave me the gym clothes she kept in the trunk of her car. The hooded top was a little big, but the leggings and crop top fit, as did the running shoes. I couldn't thank her enough. She still refused any money and gave me her phone number as well as her good luck wishes instead. I'd caught the first bus out and ended up in Phoenix. I'd been tempted to phone Special Agent Weathers and WITSEC, but when I finally reached for the payphone, I found myself calling Bono's old number instead. Hell, I'd been surprised that I remembered it, but not as surprised as I was when he answered. And now he was here, next to me, driving along the road to Colorado.

There was no question about it. Things were awkward as fuck. But a strange peace washed through me and for the first time in a very long time, I found myself relaxing. I took a deep breath, leaned my head against the rest, and closed my eyes. I only realized I must have fallen asleep when bright sunlight glared behind my closed lids and the car came to a stop.

"Are we there?" I asked, wondering how long I'd slept.

Bono smiled and shook his head. "We both need a decent rest and some food," he said and motioned out the window to a motel very similar to the one I'd just left.

"I am hungry," I said as my stomach growled.

"We'll book into a room, and I'll head across the road to grab some breakfast."

"A McGriddle sounds just about perfect right about now," I agreed. "Some coffee wouldn't go amiss either."

"We'll grab some coffee later. For now, we'll eat and rest up for a few hours."

The keycard took four swipes before it let us into the simple room. Not a promising start, but the reassuring hum of an air conditioning unit greeted me as I stepped through the door. The twin beds were clean and comfortable when I perched on the end of the first, and the scent of soap and cleaning fluid filled the air.

Bono confirmed my order, refusing my money, before leaving me alone in the room. I switched on the TV and waited with bated breath for him to return. Despite living alone for the last decade, the room felt eerily empty without Bono in it.

I jumped to my feet as soon as he got back and moved to the small table, placing our paper-wrapped food on top of it.

"Do you still ride a motorcycle?" I asked when I took the seat opposite him, despite his leather jacket implying he did so.

He grinned and shrugged off the jacket before placing it on the back of his chair. "I still ride," he said.

"What's the logo on the back all about? The moon and the skull?"

"It represents the motorcycle club I belong to. Forever Midnight. And that perfect moment of peace and stillness that comes over the world only when the moon is full. That moment where nothing else matters and you wish the feeling would last forever."

"It sounds like this club means a lot to you," I said between bitefulls. I closed my eyes and savored the delicious maple-infused pancakes, wrapped around bacon, egg, and cheese as though it was the best food in the world.

"You always did have lousy taste in food," Bono said, smiling at me over the top of his own food.

I shook my head. "If this is about the pineapple on pizza thing again, I might have to give you a slap," I said without thinking.

Bono leaned back in his chair and grinned. "Then maybe it is."

I held his gaze for a moment. He looked at me and the years were wiped away. We could be sitting in our old apartment, flirting, and having fun. The realization that we weren't had me drawing in a deep breath. I shifted my gaze back to my food and took another bite. It didn't taste as good as the first.

"Tell me about this Forever Midnight," I said to take the conversation back to safer ground. "And your move to Colorado. When did that happen?"

"After you... left, I joined the military. Did a four-year tour as a medic in Afghanistan—"

"You were in Afghanistan. You loved your job. Why would you leave it?" The question was out of my mouth before I had the chance to stop it, but Bono joining the military had surprised me. He was never one for following rules or letting himself be bossed around when I knew him.

"I needed to get as far away from L.A. as soon as possible. Enlisting seemed the quickest way to do that. A buddy of mine in the service came from Colorado. I moved there when my tour was over."

"With your buddy?" I asked.

Bono shook his head and put the last two bites of his McGriddle down on its paper. "No. His body was repatriated nineteen months earlier. I went to visit his family and grave and ended up staying."

His voice was flat and emotionless as he said the last words and a hollowness opened up in my chest. "I'm sorry," I said, discarding the last of my own food.

Bono shrugged. "It happens." He grabbed his griddle and swallowed it in two bites before standing. "We'd better rest," he said, signaling our conversation as over.

He flicked off the TV; closed the curtains, blocking out the light; and checked the door was locked before stripping naked and climbing into one of the single beds. I tried to keep my gaze averted but couldn't resist taking a glance at his tight ass and sculpted body. He'd gained more tattoos over the years, making me remember that I'd never seen the fully completed first one.

I gathered the food wrappings from the table and tossed

them into the bin before moving to the bathroom. Inside, I stripped to my panties and wrapped a towel around me. Back in the main room, I placed my folded clothes on the chair by the table and climbed into the bed. Only when I was beneath the covers did I pull the towel free and discard it to the side of the bed.

Bono rolled and faced the other side of the room with his back to me. "The Hope I knew wouldn't have acted that shy," he said into the darkness.

"The Bono I knew wouldn't have gotten a room with separate beds," I countered.

I stared at the ceiling until Bono's breathing told me he was asleep, and then turned on my side and tried to copy him. I couldn't say how much later it was when he cried out and woke me. After a few disorienting moments where my heart raced and I sat up in bed, searching the room for our attacker, I realized that Bono was still asleep.

"Tony, no," he said before making a strangled noise that made me think he might be crying.

His body thrashed on the bed, and he threw off the covers. I did the same and made my way tentatively towards him.

"Bono," I whispered when he murmured something unintelligible. "It's Hope. You're having a bad dream. There's no Tony here. Everything's fine."

"Tony's dead. Hope's dead. They're all gone," he muttered, making my chest tighten.

I sat on the bed next to him and touched his shoulder. "It is Hope," I said. "I'm not gone. I'm not gone."

Bono rolled and slipped his arms around my waist. For a second, I wondered if he'd woken up, but soon realized that wasn't the case. I debated pulling away and going back to my own bed, but Bono's arms around me felt too good. Instead, I slipped down the bed and drew my feet up to lay next to him, gathering the blanket to cover us again. His body pressed against mine, and I cherished the weighted feeling, the closeness of his heat, and the touch of his skin. I ran my hand over the corded muscles in his chest, noting the outline of his tattoos in the darkness. He shifted, somehow driving his leg between mine, and I couldn't stop the wetness that flooded to my core when I felt his erection, thick and rigid.

I buried my head beneath his chin and savored the musky scent of him, wishing I was the woman I'd once been. The woman who was brave enough to take him whenever I wanted him. But that woman was long gone.

CHAPTER FIVE

Bono

I woke to find Hope sleeping in the crook of my arm. Her naked body pressed against mine. I stared at the perfect roundness of her breasts. My cock instantly hardened. I tried not to move.

Even though the curtains were closed, I noted that it was dark outside. We must have slept all day. When we'd gone to bed, I hadn't set an alarm as I wasn't used to sleeping more than an hour or two at a time before waking up. I could honestly say, I'd had the best night's, or rather day's, sleep in ten years, and it was difficult not to associate Hope's presence with that fact.

I lay still, staring at her sleeping face and enjoying the scent of her skin, her hair. *Fuck.* She really was the most beautiful woman I'd ever seen.

I'd been all set to run away from my twelfth foster home in half the number of years when Caroline, my foster mother, had opened the door and brought Hope into my life. Even though she was only fifteen, she had more guts than anyone I'd ever met. She looked at me and winked. I decided then and there that I wasn't going anywhere.

Kate's murder must have shaken her to the core for her to allow herself to be bullied into the witness protection program.

She shifted in my arms and her eyes fluttered open. She looked at me and smiled sleepily. But then she came fully awake and jumped up, out of the bed, dragging the bedcovers with her.

Her eyes drifted to my cock, standing at full mast. I just caught a glimpse of her eyes widening before she turned her back to me. "Sorry," she said. "I... I... You were having a bad dream. I didn't mean to—"

"It's fine," I said, sitting up. "Thank you. I slept better than I have in a long time."

"Me too," was all she said before her shoulders hunched and sagged as though she was taking a deep breath. Without saying another word, she grabbed her clothes and moved to the bathroom.

I sat on the edge of the bed for a moment, listening as the shower turned on and the sound of cascading water filled the air. Trying not to think of Hope wet and naked in the room next to mine, and hating that was where my mind went, I threw on my clothes, grabbed my phone and went outside where I hoped to find a better signal.

It was ten-past-ten at night when I hit the screen to dial Cane's number.

"It's late," he said, and I realized that Thea might now be home with the baby.

"Damn it, sorry," I said. "I haven't woken the baby, have I?"

Cane huffed down the phone. "That's not what I meant. They're not coming out of the hospital until tomorrow. We've been trying to reach you all day. I was about ready to send out a fucking search party."

I glanced at my phone and noted the missed messages. "Reception was bad in the room," I said. "We stopped at a motel to get some rest and slept all day."

"Yeah, you *slept* all day."

I shook my head but decided to ignore the mockery in his tone. "I hardly fucking believe it myself, but that's what happened."

"You need to get on the road as soon as possible. Whatever fucking connection Jameson has in New York has told him that this Dolmilo guy is sending people out to try and locate Hope. You're included as a possible contact to check out. Where are you?"

"A little outside of Santa Fe."

"That's what, a five, six-hour drive?"

The night was quiet and the road clear. We could grab a

drive-through to speed things up. I leaned my back against the balcony railing and looked at the door to our room. Hopefully, Hope would be out of the shower now. I could take five minutes to clean up, and then we could be out of here. "About that," I said, agreeing with Bono's estimate relating to our travel time.

"Okay. I'm gonna get some brothers to meet you on the I-25 as you drive by Pueblo. Until then, you're on your own. Move as fast as you can, and go to the clubhouse, not your cabin."

I sighed and shook my head. "You really think this is necessary?" I asked, hoping he was being overly cautious.

"Jameson seems to think it is, and I've never been inclined to ignore his judgment. Now shift your ass into fucking gear and move."

Despite the situation, I smiled when I ended the call. Cane had only cussed twice during the entire conversation. Thea was rubbing off on him and making him a changed man in more ways than one.

I turned back to the door and took a deep breath, trying to ease the tension building in my shoulders, before reentering the motel room. Hope was still in the bathroom, so I knocked on the door.

"We gotta move," I said, deciding it best not to share anything Cane had said with her. She was worried enough as it was. If she knew Dolmilo was likely waiting to see if she turned up at my place, she might consider running as her only option. But I'd be damned if I was going to let that happen. As far as I was concerned, Dolmilo was the walking fucking corpse, not Hope.

She was fully dressed and dabbing her wet hair to dry it when she opened the bathroom door. She looked at me with wary eyes, and once again, confusion rolled through me. We'd been engaged, and as close as two people could be. But what was there for us now? I'd wished for Hope's return, that the events of that night had turned out differently, every day that followed them. Now that I'd been granted my wish, things were no clearer than they were before. Not for the first time, I wondered how much she'd changed. There was the obvious knock to her self-confidence, but what else lay beneath the surface? I would always love Hope, but had that love changed from what it once was? The stirring in my cock every time I looked at her showed that my body wanted her as much as it always had.

"We need to move," I said, shaking the thoughts from my head. "I'm gonna take two minutes to shower up, and then we're out of here. Don't leave the room." I pushed my way into the bathroom when she nodded.

Within ten minutes we were going through the drive-through and grabbing coffee and burgers before heading out on the road.

CHAPTER SIX

Hope

I sipped at my coffee and looked out the window. Not a night had gone by in the last three days where I hadn't been chugging down a road, whether on a bus or in a car, staring into the darkness outside but not really seeing anything.

The events had all been a blur from the second I walked into The Chandlery and saw Mickey Dolmilo at the bar until now. Even sitting in the car, watching the world go by, I wasn't entirely convinced events were real. Only Bono's rock-solid presence next to me said that they were. Hell, for all I knew, the guy at the bar was just a Dolmilo look-alike and I'd run away for no reason. I had been thinking about moving on and also about my past a lot lately. Maybe I conjured him as an excuse to get back in touch with Bono.

I scoffed and shook my head.

Bono glanced at me and raised an eyebrow. I wanted nothing more than to reach out and touch his perfect face.

"What are you thinking?" he asked me.

I leaned my head back against the headrest and took another sip of coffee. "I was just thinking how great it was to see you and wondering if Dolmilo was still safely locked away in prison, and I'd conjured his image as an excuse to see you."

The corner of Bono's lips lifted in a smile and he looked at me with eyes that saw way too much under his lashes. It faltered, making my heart drop into my stomach, and he turned his gaze back to the road ahead. "As much as I wish that was true," he said. "One of my brothers confirmed he was out on appeal." He cleared his throat and stared dead ahead as though there was more to what he knew but wasn't ready to share it with me.

"Brothers?" I questioned to keep him talking.

"From Forever Midnight."

"Your motorcycle club. You never did tell me about them."

"Not much to tell that you won't learn as soon as you meet them. Much like the soldiers in my platoon, they would lay down their lives to protect mine and any other brothers. We stand and fight as one unit."

"So, you went from me to the military to Forever Midnight." I huffed out a breath and took another sip of coffee, feeling somewhat wistful. "Always searching for the family you never had as a child."

Bono almost growled and his hands tightened on the

steering wheel. "I had all the family I ever wanted with you, and I didn't *go* from you to the military. You went from me."

I hated hearing the condemnation in his words, but he was right. I left, and Bono lost even more people after that. No wonder he hated me for it, even while I still loved him.

The silence stretched between us. The weather shifted and the skies covered us in a fine mist of rain, distorting the view of the road. Soon, the deluge increased, and Bono had to turn the wipers on. I sat listening to their incessant swish until Bono suddenly shifted in his seat. "What about you?" he asked. "How have the past ten years been for you in witness protection?"

"Lonely," I answered. Bono only nodded his head in response, and I wasn't sure if he was agreeing I'd been lonely or that he had too. "I was on a flight from L.A. to Washington within three hours of Kate's murder. They kept me there for a little over two weeks. For the next year, while the trial was running, I never spent more than a couple of weeks in one place."

"Were you at the trial?" Bono asked.

"No. I testified remotely." I tipped my cup up to get the last drip of coffee and placed it in the cupholder. "After the conviction, I was settled in Nebraska. But there were rumors Dolmilo had located me. After that, there was Georgia, Michigan. Texas and Utah. I never really got to stay in one place for more than a few years."

"Sounds hard," he said.

"It wasn't easy. More than anything, like I said, it was lonely."

Bono's brow furrowed and he stared ahead at the road again. "Why were you moved so much?" he asked after a moment. "Was your position compromised each time?" I nodded. "Doesn't that seem strange to you? Did you ever contact someone out of your old life, someone who could point their finger in your direction?"

I huffed and closed my eyes, leaning my head against the headrest. The steady swoosh of the wipers and the drumming of the rain on the window made my head hurt and made it feel as though there was nothing outside the bubble of our car. "Who else did I have but you?" I asked, unable to keep the pain from my voice.

Bono was silent for a long time, thinking things through and choosing his words carefully, the way he always liked to. We were both so different, and yet completely the same. When he did finally speak, his voice was soft and full of concern. "All the evidence against Dolmilo was either lost or destroyed. I don't know what evidence they held against him, but I'm damn certain they would have needed to keep it while he ran through his appeals process."

"I made a video recording of Kate's murder on my phone," I said and shifted uncomfortably when Bono's eyes darted toward me.

"You could have been killed," he said. "Why would you risk such a thing?"

I shrugged. "I couldn't help Kate. I guess I just did what I could."

"The video would have been kept," Bono said.

I nodded. "Where are you going with this?" I asked.

"Just trying to make sense of things."

"Good luck with that."

A small smile crept onto his lips at my tone, and he reached into his jacket and pulled his phone out.

He handed it to me and asked me to call someone named Rex, and to put the call on speaker.

"Bono," Rex said as soon as he answered. "You just caught me. I'm here with Caleb, Cane, and Lucky. We were about to leave with some others to meet you by Pueblo."

"I need you to stay at home and work on something else for me." Bono raised his voice to be heard over the curtain of rain that pounded the car.

"Not a problem," he said. "I'm putting you on speaker."

"Bono. What do you need?" another voice asked over the line.

"I need Rex to dig into the missing files in the Dolmilo case and see what turns up."

"I doubt there'll be much," Rex said.

"I do too, but if you can get a possible date of when they went missing, that may be a start. Who was your handler in WITSEC?" he asked, turning his attention to me.

"Special Agent Craig Weathers," I answered.

Bono squinted as a set of lights grew brighter behind us, filling the car with a blinding glare.

"Fuck," Bono said.

"What is it?" a third voice shouted over the open line.

"We're not alone." The last words were barely out of Bono's mouth when the vehicle behind us clipped the rear bumper.

Bono wrestled with the wheel and got the car under control. I screamed when the car behind bumped us again. This time, when our car swerved, we skidded sideways towards the guardrail.

"Rex," Bono shouted, reminding me that we were still on a call. "Trace us. Now. We're going over." He gave me a tight-lipped smile. "Hold tight."

The sound as we crashed through the guardrail would haunt me in much the same way the gunshots that killed Kate had. It was followed by the whoosh of the airbags as they deployed. Although we were doing at least sixty, for a frightful second, time stood still, and we were trapped in a moment where the front of the car was in the air and the back still on the road. I screamed, but the sound was muffled by the bag in my face and the rain. My bag deflated and I was able to glance at Bono. He wrestled to get his own out of the way and return his hands to the steering wheel. Clasping on, he looked for any way he could to guide us to safety. If I were a better person, I'd feel regret for dragging Bono into my problems and putting him in this situation, but mostly I was just glad that if I was about to die, at least I got to see him one more time.

In the darkness, everything was a flash of confusion. The right headlight went out with the first jarring impact. We headed into a tangle of shrubs and careened down the steep incline, out of control, pinned to our seats by our belts. Stones, branches, and rocky mounds of mud pummeled the tires and the underside of our car. We hit something and the car spun on its axis. My breathing came in shallow gasps, and my body felt heavy. I was too stunned to move or even think when we finally came to a stop.

"Are you hurt?" Bono asked, instantly moving. When I didn't respond, he unclipped his belt and shifted to face me. He took my head in his hands and stared into my eyes before looking up and down my body. "Are you hurt?" he asked again.

I shook my head and shifted. A shot rang out and a voice shouted along the still open line. Bono unclipped my belt and delved between my legs to grab his phone.

"We have to move." He kicked open his door and came around to my side of the car. Headlights shimmered through the rain and illuminated the sky from above, but we were in complete darkness. Bono wrestled with my door for a few seconds before wrapping his elbow in his jacket, smashing my window, and helping me climb through. A second shot rang out. Its echo reverberated through the canyon like thunder. Someone shouted to grab the night vision goggles. Bono pulled me down to shelter by the side of the car. We crouched in the mud. Bono shook out his leather jacket and placed it over my shoulders to help keep the worst of the rain from seeping into my clothes.

"They're firing blindly, but that won't be the case for much longer," he said while I threaded my arms through the sleeves.

"Bono." The voice on the other end of the line made me jump.

"We're still here, Cane."

"We've got your location. Pull the battery from your phone. Rex said that they probably traced your location through it the same way we have. Hide. Stay back from the sight of the road, but don't lose your bearings. We're on our way."

"Got ya. See you soon, brothers."

"You bet you fucking will. Stay safe."

Without waiting for another word, Bono ended the call and pulled both the battery and SIM from his phone before pocketing them.

"It's not gonna be easy in the dark, and we're at a distinct disadvantage, but we've got to move. You ready?"

I took a deep breath to steel my nerves and looked up to the headlights above us again, raising my hand and blinking through the swollen drops. The incline was as steep as I'd imagined as we'd bounced down into the canyon. With the jagged rocks and outcroppings, it was a miracle we weren't dead or at least severely maimed in some way. But apart from a few bruises that weren't even worth mentioning, I was unscathed, and Bono looked to be the same.

Bono held his hand out to me, and I took it. "Keep low," he said as he pulled me to my feet and dragged me towards the scant tree line.

CHAPTER SEVEN

Bono

We raced along a barely-there trail, the muddy ground grasping at our feet and making Hope slip.

"This way," I said and reassured her that I doubted our attackers would climb down the cliff and pursue us further. The best thing we could do was get as far away from the area as quickly as possible.

My eyes adapted to what little light there was, but from the way Hope dragged her feet, she was obviously struggling. The flimsy running shoes she wore were not up to the task they faced. Without my jacket I had no doubt she'd be shivering by now. Not that the limited protection that provided would do her much good for long. We had to find shelter and fast.

"I feel like I'm wading through a swamp," she said and cast a wary glance back. "Or a minefield." Despite her attempt to make her words light, tension poured from her with every step, as though she were either waiting to trip and be laid flat by a crag, or worse, a bullet.

I squeezed her hand tighter and hoped that my assessment of her physical state had been correct. There was no time to check her over thoroughly at the car, and it was difficult to get a good read on her given the weather. But her eye movement had been controlled and measured and she'd followed my actions with no problems. For now, I'd ruled out the possibility of a concussion. Which was always a worry when an airbag deployed.

When I was satisfied that we were far enough away from the road, and I could no longer see any lights, I pulled us to a stop while making a map in my head.

From the sounds, and the brief glimpse I'd managed of our pursuers, I estimated that three guys were in the car that rammed us off the road. Although I couldn't be sure that any were Dolmilo. If I was by myself, I would have risked trying to take them out, but I couldn't leave Hope alone and unprotected in the rain. She'd been through enough already. She was trying to be brave, but the Hope I knew was a city girl through and through. She wasn't one for camping and had little hope of surviving in the wilderness without help. Hell, neither of us would without a fire and shelter.

Although, I reminded myself, I'd have to revise that assessment. She was always resourceful. And she'd evaded

Dolmilo when he murdered Kate ten years ago, and then again a few days ago. I shook my head. Running through a city and a built-up suburban area was one thing, stumbling through the trees and mountains in the pouring rain was something completely different.

"Do you think they're following us?" Hope asked after a moment.

Despite my earlier conviction that they wouldn't, I thought about her question. They'd mentioned night vision goggles, but it was doubtful they had the equipment to make it down the slope. Hell, they probably thought our chances of walking away from the crash were slim to none. As we'd hit the guardrail, I'd thought the same myself. If the car had flipped, there's no doubt we'd be goners.

No. It was more likely they had already checked me out and had the number of every one of my brothers. Instead of chasing us blindly into the great beyond, it would make more sense for them to wait for me to contact someone from home and get a new location for us.

I took a deep breath and looked at Hope. The furrow in her brow had returned, but even in the dark through the rain, I could see the rest she'd had at the motel had banished the worst of the dark circles under her eyes. God, I wanted to pull her into my arms and tell her that everything would be alright. But how could I? There was too much time between us, too much life we'd lived apart.

"We need to find shelter. When we were driving, I noticed a rocky outcropping on the other side of the road where we might find some small caves or, at least, a ledge we can take cover under until my brothers arrive." Before I'd finished speaking the words, Hope was shaking her head, no. "It's the best option. You have to trust me, okay?"

Hope shuddered, but her eyes never left my own. "I trust you." She nodded, smiled, and stood tall.

It was as if a switch had been flicked inside her head. A new energy filled her. She may be scared, wet, and cold, but she was my sexy, stubborn soldier. All she ever needed in life was a plan. I'd seen it a million times. With no direction, she would stumble around like a lost lamb, but the second she'd decided on an action, she focused all her energy on it and wouldn't stop until that goal was reached. Thinking of this reminded me of her plans to return to college all those years ago. I hoped she'd managed to fulfill that dream. It would have eaten her up inside to have abandoned it.

If my estimations and spatial awareness were on point, we were a good mile behind where we went off the road when we approached the incline leading back up to the interstate.

"Okay," I said after finding us the best spot to start climbing.

"We're going to climb up here. And when we reach the top, we're going to make sure the coast is clear and then make a run for the other side of the road. Don't stop. Don't look back. When we're across we'll look for that shelter."

"And if we can't find any?"

"Then we'll hike north, following the road at a distance."

She nodded and smiled weakly. We both knew we were still a good three hours out of Castle Rock. More than enough time to get hypothermia. The rain was easing, but that wouldn't help dry our clothes.

We trudged up the gravel incline and braced ourselves for the more difficult climb ahead. It wouldn't be easy, given the poor light and the wet surface. It would also leave us fully exposed should our attackers still be around. My hairs bristled at the thought of Hope getting hurt, but having assessed the situation, I knew we had no other choice.

"Are you ready?" I asked.

"As I'll ever be."

I gave her hand another squeeze and pointed up the rock face to where the best hand and footholds could be found. "You're going up first. I'll be right behind you." I'd be better able to guide her from behind, and hopefully, grab her if she fell. "When you reach the top, lie flat on the ground and don't move."

"Lie flat. Don't move." Without another word, she reached

for the first handhold and climbed.

Despite my worries, she made her way easily upward, and I found myself relaxing and admiring the shape of her bottom in the leggings. When a rock came away beneath my foot and I had to scramble for another purchase, I decided it was best to focus on the task at hand and not Hope's delectable rear.

When I reached the top, Hope was flat on the ground just as I'd instructed. I did the same and surveyed the area. There was no sign of anyone or any vehicle. Of course, there was always the possibility that the car had driven off, leaving one man behind to see if we returned and take us out, but my instincts told me that wasn't the case.

"Okay. It looks clear. We're gonna make a run for it. You see those rocks to the right—" I pointed at an outcropping that looked to provide the best shelter in the distance. "When I say go, head there as fast as you can," I said when Hope nodded. "Okay, go."

Hope didn't hesitate, she took off like a soldier trained to follow commands. And she was fast. Faster than I could hope to be. I'd kept in shape over the years; the shape of Hope's body had shown me she had too. Even more so the way she moved now. She hopped over a boulder as easily as a gymnast.

I couldn't help the grin that spread across my face when I joined her.

"I think I spotted a good place to shelter," she said, matching my grin.

"Great. You lead the way and I'll keep a look out." Within ten minutes, Hope had led me to a group of large boulders with a nook leading to a cavernous space large enough to house six men between them.

CHAPTER EIGHT

Hope

As soon as we were sheltered from the elements, the rain eased. Typical.

It felt strange to be sitting beneath the boulders with Bono. When we arrived, he'd made himself busy. First by digging two holes in the ground to one side of our shelter, and then he left for a short time to gather what little dry kindling and wood he could before asking me for the small cylindrical plastic box he kept in his inside pocket. He unscrewed the lid, produced a match from inside, and proceeded to light a fire in the larger of the holes.

"Won't the smoke and flames be seen from the road?" I asked.

Bono shook his head. "I checked the road when gathering the wood. They're gone. Even so, this is a Dakota fire pit. The flames are underground in the hole and because of the chimney pit," he said, pointing to the second hole, "it burns hot and steady, reducing the output of smoke."

Within minutes the fire was going, and I could sense the heat filling our nook. Bono asked me for a small mirror he kept in another pocket and used it as a means to direct the light from the fire into our corner of the nook. After that, he knelt by my side and gave me a once-over.

"I told you, I'm fine. I've nothing more than a few scrapes and bruises."

"We both need to get out of these wet clothes," he said, his voice serious despite the cheeky grin that played on his lips. "If we lay them on the ground by the fire, they might dry out a bit before my brothers arrive."

"How will we know when they get here?" I asked, still finding it strange that he referred to his club friends as brothers.

"We'll hear them." He dragged me to my feet and lifted his shirt, cleaning his hands on the wet fabric before tossing it close to the fire. "I'm sorry. I don't have a towel on hand."

Without saying a word, I handed him his jacket while trying not to look at his broad chest, sleek with muscle. I lifted the hooded top over my head and placed it on the ground by the fire. Heat emanated from the floor and suddenly our space felt far too hot. My leggings followed, as did Bono's jeans. He sat on the ground, butt ass naked, and patted his jacket laid out next to him. I sat on it before removing my crop top, bra, and panties, and tossing them closer to the fire while drawing my knees up.

All the while, I could sense Bono's smirk even while not looking at his face.

My chest tightened, and my skin flushed, and for once, it was nothing to do with worry or fear. We may have been in a car crash an hour or so earlier, and Dolmilo may be out there waiting to kill me — in fact, it was a safe bet he was, even if he wasn't directly outside our nook — but I couldn't seem to care at that moment in time.

Bono wrapped his arm around me. It felt so good, too good. Having his bare skin touching mine, feeling the warmth of his presence. I allowed myself to close my eyes and rest my head on his shoulder. If I wished hard enough, I could almost imagine the years washing away.

He shifted closer still and skimmed the back of his fingers over my cheek, turning my head to face him. I opened my eyes. Orange light flickered over Bono's face. A small voice inside my head told me to resist, that this was a bad idea, a *very* bad idea. But his solid presence struck a deep yearning in the center of my core. Every part of him called to me like some strange magnetic pull. My body and soul needed him, to feel his lips and his body pressed against mine, the touch of his cock at my entrance.

He trailed his fingers over my lips. I opened my mouth slightly. He pushed his finger inside and I tasted the fresh, earthy scent of the rain. I bit his finger softly, and he laughed. I smiled.

Arousal flared in eyes that never left my own as he withdrew his finger and ran the tip over my lips.

I moistened them further with the tip of my tongue and held his gaze. My heart hammered and my breathing was ragged. Bono cut my oxygen completely off as he pressed his lips against mine. The taste of him was like a powerful drug, drawing me deeper into an enticing fantasy. His tongue darted between my lips in a kiss that was all-consuming.

He pulled back, looking at me again, right into my eyes. "My Hope."

His words made my body ache with sheer pleasure.

He slipped his hand around the back of my head into my hair, and he pulled me forward, devouring my mouth again. Moisture built between my thighs.

I pictured myself on my knees before him and moaned. I wanted so much to suck on his dick and see if it tasted as good as I remembered. Years of stress could be washed away in just a few moments with Bono.

"I missed you," I said.

"Not as much as I missed you," he echoed in my ear, his hot breath like fire on my sensitive skin.

I grabbed his free hand and pressed it between my legs. He smiled and I felt myself become a puddle in his hands. He pinched my clit between his fingers, clasping on tight. I whimpered; my every nerve endings prickled in pleasure.

He moved his hand from my hair and roved over my thigh and up to my breast. He cupped it and tweaked my hard nipple as his other hand remained clamped on the swollen bud of my clit.

My head fell back, and I gasped. "Oh, my God." I closed my eyes, enjoying the sensation, and squirmed needing more.

"I want you," I said.

"I'm yours to command," he whispered, never letting go.

"I... I thought we agreed it was my turn to be yours."

Bono laughed. "In that case, show me how much you want me."

I opened my eyes and pulled back. Bono let me go. The release of his touch on my clit and nipple hit me like a great loss, but I smiled, leaned back, and spread my legs. All the shyness I'd built over the years flushed from my system. With Bono, I'd always been who I was meant to be.

I trailed my hand up over my stomach and cupped my breast. Bono rested against the wall with a smile on his face and watched me. I brushed my thumb over my nipple and relished the flip-flopping of the butterflies in my belly. I did what I'd done countless times before and imagined Bono's touch.

"Not a single orgasm I've brought myself to over the years could be done without imagining it was your touch I felt instead of my own."

Bono's eyes drifted between my legs, and I spread them wider for him to see. I stroked and teased my clit for a while circling the nub before pushing my finger inside. "Every single time, I touch myself I think of you."

I focused on Bono's face as my fingers plunged in and out of my core. His eyes twinkled with mischief in the firelight.

"Who did you think about when you were with other men?" Bono asked, his voice teasing.

"I only ever think of you," I said, choosing not to take the question to heart and allow it to spoil the mood. I wasn't going to lie and say there had been no other men. When I'd first left, I thought I could lose myself in sex, that I could find someone who did to me all that Bono did. But that fantasy soon fled. "Your hands on my skin, your mouth sucking my nipples, your cock buried dead inside me." I moaned, wishing for all those things to happen now, knowing that they could.

Bono shifted forward. His hand rested on mine before pinching my clit while I continued to finger-fuck myself. I nearly lost it when he pressed his finger tight against mine and joined me.

"Was this your fantasy?" he asked.

"No," I growled and looked into his eyes. "I always wanted more."

"Was that a request?" he asked and moved his head between

my legs. "I thought you were mine to command."

Without saying another word, he withdrew my fingers and lifted them to his mouth, sucking off my wetness.

I jolted when he circled his fingers around my throbbing bud and arched my back into the sensation.

Still holding my hand, he pushed it behind my back, making me arch further. Holding it in place, he teased my nipple with his tongue, sucking it in before nipping it, all while his fingers teased my clit and slid deep into my core.

I yelped when he gave my nipple a quick, sharp bite. He shifted and took my clit into his mouth, sucking and nipping at the hard bud. He licked my slit and delved inside with his tongue before returning his focus to my clit.

My breath became fast and labored. My hips rocked in time to his penetrating fingers. Sensations bloomed within me. "Oh, fuck, Bono."

My core clenched and spasmed around his fingers. He let go of my hand and cupped my breast, groping as my wetness streamed around his fingers and into his mouth. He welcomed it, and I moaned deeply as he licked and sucked me dry.

"Oh, fuck, is right," he said, but he didn't stop. He swirled his tongue over my clit and pounded me with his fingers until he made me come apart all over again.

"Fuck, Bono. I-I can't," I said, doing my best not to scream.

While I was still shuddering with my climax, he guided his big, thick cock to my sopping entrance and pushed inside. My legs wrapped around him as if they had a mind of their own and were never going to let him go.

"Was this your fantasy?" he asked again.

I laughed between desperate gasps. "I… oh, fuck… I'll always want more."

I bit my lip and moaned as he fulfilled my wishes, thrusting deeper and deeper inside me, filling me up and taking my breath away.

CHAPTER NINE

Bono

We lay in the warmth of our hidey-hole and talked about events that we'd missed in each other's lives over the years.

"Did you ever go to college?"

"Hope Fisher never got to go," she said as I glanced at the sky, lightening through the opening that led outside. "But Hope Francois managed to stay in one place long enough to gain a marketing degree. Not that she ever got to use it, that honor was passed on to Hope Fox."

"Hope Fox. I like that, though it doesn't sound as good as Hope Travers." My voice trailed at the end when Hope shifted beside me, and I remembered our engagement and all the plans we'd made for our wedding. "Did you always get to keep your first name?" I asked to shift the focus of our conversation somewhere else.

"They said that keeping the same name helps people to

adjust better to their new life. If someone called out Hope and I reacted, it would be a little awkward if that wasn't my first name in whatever identity I had taken on."

I stroked her hair behind her ear and breathed deeply, wondering how difficult things must have been, but more so, how complicated I had made them now. It was just, being with her, and seeing the Hope I remembered shining through, had taken me back to old times. To a time when it was just me and Hope, and the rest of the world didn't matter. I guess that time was my Forever Midnight. My moment of happiness and peace, and I wanted to go back there. A part of me wanted to stay in the shelter of these boulders forever. At least then, we could pretend that we were back where we used to be instead of two lost souls who'd found each other for a moment's respite. "Why the same initials?" I asked, realizing that each of her surnames had started with the letter 'F', in the same way hers had.

"That's in case you find yourself signing your old name somewhere. Having the same last initial gives you a little time to catch your mistake and remedy it before completing the signature."

I smiled. "They think of everything."

Hope sighed at this and propped herself up on her elbow to look at me. "Do they? I was thinking about what you said earlier about all my identities being compromised. You know, when I saw Dolmilo—" she sucked in a breath and shook her head "—as well as feeling sheer terror, I initially dismissed calling the Marshals as they were the only people who could have given away my location to Dolmilo. I can't help but think that was the case each and every time."

"If that were the case, one of his men would have tried to kill you before now. Plus, why would the Marshals have been so quick to relocate you the other times?"

Hope scoffed. "Maybe he wants to kill me himself. I cost him ten years of his life. I'm pretty pissed at him for costing me ten years of mine." With that, she laced her fingers between mine and put her head back down. "I'm not saying that everyone at WITSEC is on his payroll, but all it takes is one bad egg."

I nodded and was about to say that Rex and possibly Jameson with his contacts would be able to find out when the faint rumbling of bikes filled the air.

Hope instantly stiffened, jumping up, and coming to attention as though ready to bolt.

I smiled at her naked perfection but sighed inwardly that our time in this bubble had come to an end. "It's fine. I told you we'd hear when Forever Midnight arrived."

Hope visibly relaxed, grabbed my clothes, and threw them at me, and then tugged on her own. "Thank fuck, they're dry," she said. "I was so not looking forward to putting them on damp."

We emerged into the bright sunlight a few seconds later. The motorcycles had come to a stop a fair distance up the road. I could just make out Cane among the twenty plus riders who'd come to find us.

As we moved closer, I noticed Caleb standing by the broken guardrail, pointing down at the car. Lucky jumped out of his jeep and started hauling rope from the back. They must have been planning on climbing down to try and find us. Cane spotted me and Hope walking down the road. He called to the others and every head turned our way.

Hope fidgeted uncomfortably beside me, and I couldn't help but chuckle. "They're not as bad as they look," I said.

She smiled and cast them another wary glance, but she stopped fidgeting.

"How the fuck did you two walk away from that?" Cane said as soon as we were within earshot while pointing down to the wreckage of our rental car. "You're like a cat with nine lives."

I looked at Hope and considered how lucky she especially was to be alive. "Let's hope so," I said. "We'd better get this car moved before the police find it and start asking questions. We'll need to report the damage to the rental company too."

"I'll take care of that," Lucky said. "You'd all better get back on the road and somewhere safe."

Caleb agreed. Lucky handed Cane the keys to his jeep, and

Cane gave him the keys to his bike. I guessed that meant the three of us would be traveling back to Castle Rock together.

"You sure you should be out here?" I asked Cane when he started the engine, and we headed toward home. I sat up front with him while Hope opted to sit alone in the back. She'd barely said a word since my brothers had arrived, and only nodded in greeting when I'd introduced them. "What time is Thea due home?"

"Not until later this afternoon," Cane responded.

I glanced in the visor mirror and saw Hope staring out the window. She seemed to be assessing everything we passed as though looking for any threats that may be following outside, and I wondered if this was a trait she'd picked up over the last ten years. Rightly so, given that Dolmilo was out there searching for a way to end her at this very moment.

CHAPTER TEN

Hope

I was exhausted by the time we arrived at the Forever Midnight clubhouse, as Bono called it. It looked like a warehouse-style building. It had security gates and a large lot with more motorcycles than I'd ever seen in one place. The ones accompanying our jeep only added to that number.

It had been strange listening to Bono and his friend Cane talk on the journey, but I was beginning to see why Bono would refer to him as his brother. The banter they shared and their obvious concern for one another had brought the years between us crashing back down. When we were alone, I could pretend that life was the way it used to be. Now, surrounded by strangers who were as close to Bono as I had ever been, made me feel depressingly alone.

It was something of a relief when the clubhouse door opened, and a blonde woman ran outside with a little girl of around three or four. The intimidation factor of all the bikers surrounding me dropped a little. They headed straight for the man Bono had introduced as Cane's blood-brother and gave him a quick hug before turning their attention to me.

"Daddy said you were in a terrible car accident," the little girl said when she reached me. It took a moment for me to process her words given the background voices and the fact that they were spoken at the speed of light. "Your clothes are dirty, but you don't look like you've been in an accident." With that, she put her hands on her hips and pouted while giving me an assessing stare.

I glanced down at my mud and dust-covered clothes and crouched to her level. "We were. Bono and me. But we're both fine thanks to your daddy and everyone else coming to help us."

"Charlie," the blonde woman said. "Let Uncle Bono's friend settle in before you ask her a million questions." She placed her hand on Charlie's shoulder and smiled at me. "It's nice to meet you," she said. "I'm Amber, and as you might have guessed, this is Charlie. You must be Hope."

"It's a pleasure to meet you, Amber."

She sighed and looked at the clubhouse. "You must be exhausted. I wasn't sure about your size, but I put a few clothes in one of the spare rooms for you to try out, and now that I've seen you, I can grab you some more clothes for later."

"Thank you, that's really too much."

"Not at all."

I glanced at Bono who was talking with Cane and his brother. Another man had joined them. I studied Bono's face and saw how at ease he was in their company, although he seemed most at ease with Cane.

He was always the most ruggedly handsome man I'd ever seen, and that hadn't changed even with him surrounded by his none-too-shabby biker friends — seriously, it should be illegal for so many gorgeous men to be standing so close together. If they took their shirts off, I'd think I'd gone to watch Magic Mike with Danielle again, but with way more tattoos.

Bono caught me looking and gave me a nod and a smile that I knew he meant to be reassuring. But the truth was, now that I was here, surrounded by strangers, I felt anything but reassured. I had no idea where we went from here. It was not that I expected to be whisked back to Bono's place and spend the entire time alone with him. Hell, for all I knew, this was where Bono lived. I just couldn't help but think whatever we'd found in the nook was gone.

"Let's go inside," Amber said, bringing me out of my thoughts. "I'll show you to the room so you can get some rest. You must be exhausted."

"I am. But I have to be honest, I'm not sure I could sleep without some food. I don't suppose there's a kitchen in there where I can grab a bite to eat?"

"Of course, there is, silly," Charlie said, grabbing my hand, dragging me into the building, and bringing a smile to my face.

She led me through a large open area with what looked like a bar at one end and to a kitchen in the back. She took great joy in sitting me on a bar stool while she went to the fridge. Amber motioned for the few men inside to leave.

Only when Charlie pulled out a bottle of beer did Amber step in. "That is not food, no matter what Daddy pretends." She grabbed the bottle and put it back.

I glanced at the clock on the wall and noted it was only nine-thirty in the morning. If it wasn't for that fact, truth be told, a cold beer wouldn't have gone amiss. Although on my empty stomach, it would have hit me harder than I would have liked.

"Will bacon and eggs be okay?" she asked. "They don't tend to keep anything healthy in here."

"Sounds great," I replied. "So, um… you're Caleb's wife. Have I got that right?"

Amber froze in front of the fridge with a pack of bacon in her hands. "Caleb's wife. I don't think I'll ever stop smiling when people call me that," she said. "It's only been two weeks since we married in a small ceremony."

Charlie scrambled onto the stool next to mine. "We live with Daddy now. He lets me sit on his motorcycle, and I have a new bedroom with dolphins on the wall."

"Well, that all sounds very exciting," I said, drawn in by her enthusiasm.

"And Uncle Cane and Aunt Thea had a baby girl. And they're going to name her Buttons."

"Charlie-baby, we've been through this. They are not going to name their baby Buttons, so I don't want you to be too disappointed when it doesn't happen."

"I don't know," I laughed. "I think Buttons is a fab name."

Charlie leaned in close and whispered, covering her mouth to make sure her mom couldn't see her lips. "Uncle Cane said to pretend Buttons because Daddy'll get me a puppy." She pulled back sharply and cast Amber a nervous glance, before drawing her hands onto her lap and giggling.

I laughed again. "That sounds like a very good plan," I whispered back.

Before I had the chance to say anything else, the door opened, and Bono walked in with Cane, Caleb, and a man they introduced as Rex.

"Nice to meet you," Rex said and pulled me in for a big hug.

Bono pulled a strained face, and I smiled inwardly that he still had a possessive side toward me.

"Bono, how about some bacon and eggs?" Amber asked while flashing me a knowing look.

"Sounds great. I'm famished." He walked over to the coffee machine and offered everyone a cup. Even Charlie said yes until her mom put a stop to it and poured her a glass of milk instead. "We're gonna need to talk a bit in Caleb's office before we get some shut-eye," he said, by way of explanation for the coffee.

I looked around the room and shrank into my stool a little. "I am sorry to cause you so much trouble," I said.

Amber plated up the eggs and bacon and gave one of the servings to me along with a knife and fork. She smiled. "They're used to it. I have no idea what it is about these men, but trust me when I say that they have a pathological need to rescue women in distress." She wrapped her arm around Caleb. "It feeds their hero complex."

"Is that what we're calling it now?" he asked and kissed her on the forehead.

"That was what Thea said, and she would know, she's learning all about these mental disorders."

"So, it's a mental disorder now, too," he said, pulling back and giving her a mock stern look.

"As long as you're my hero first and foremost, does it matter?" she asked.

He kissed her again and I glanced at Bono. He'd finished giving everyone a coffee and was delving into the second plate of bacon and eggs. I swallowed a mouthful of my own food, wishing for all the world, I had twice as much more. It felt like an age since we'd grabbed a burger. But with the food settling into my stomach, washed down by the coffee, I was beginning to take more note of my dirty clothes.

Bono must have sensed my discomfort, as he quickly finished his food. "Hope and I are going up to my room to freshen up." He stood and held out his hand to me. "Leave the dishes and I'll clean them later."

"Don't worry, I've got them," Amber said. "I've taken the day off work and it will be nice to keep busy."

Bono nodded his thanks to her and told the others we'd see them in Caleb's office in twenty minutes.

CHAPTER ELEVEN

Bono

"How you doing?" I asked as I practically dragged Hope from the kitchen and up the stairs. I hated to think of her here in the room I'd shared with too many dolly girls to count but she'd started to go pale in the kitchen and I sensed she needed to get away from everyone for a little while. I took some small comfort in the fact that none of my encounters in the room had been recent and the covers were fresh and clean, and also that the club was under strict rules. No dolly girls were permitted to come around during the day. Not since Caleb had taken to bringing Charlie here on days Amber had to work.

"It's all a little overwhelming," she said as her eyes darted around the great hall and at the men sitting at the bar. "Do you really live here?"

I barked out a laugh. "No-one actually lives here. Although you'd never realize it. There always seems to be someone around. Some guys stay in the bunk room from time to time. For others, there are a couple of rooms upstairs they use when they um… need to, but a few of us have our own space. I have a cabin out in the mountains, I call home. The others thought it best not to go there in case Dolmilo already had my home address."

"I see," was all she answered.

I opened the door to my room and pulled her inside before heading to the closet. "There aren't a lot of bottoms I can offer you at the moment, but I have a T-shirt you can wear. The shower's that way if you want to freshen up."

"Amber mentioned that she's left some clothes I could try out in a spare room."

I popped out for a few minutes to retrieve the clothes, and Hope grabbed a dress and some underwear and headed into the shower room when I returned.

I sat and wondered what the fuck was wrong with me. Hope was becoming more and more withdrawn from me, and I wasn't helping. Walking into the kitchen and seeing her smiling at Charlie had brought a smile to my own face, but that fled as quickly as hers did when she saw me.

Hero complex. What a fucking joke! I didn't know how to help, especially as I was a large part of the problem.

~

We joined Caleb and the others in his office feeling at least a little cleaner, even if bed was still beckoning. He leaned back in his chair and stared at Hope. He'd changed a lot in the last month or so since Amber had come back into his life. He was happier and more easy-going than I'd ever seen him. Cane said he was back to the man he was before his father died and Amber left, but I'd only known him for a short time before that. Despite everything that had happened between them — her leaving him for four years and not even telling him about Charlie — they picked up right where they left off. Within weeks they were married and enjoying their life together. I didn't know how the fuck he could do it.

"Jameson's headed to New York," Caleb said, shuffling some papers around his desk. "He knows a few people who might be able to put a stop to Dolmilo's crusade against you."

Lucky shook his head. "We really need to learn more about that quiet fucker," he said, and I couldn't help but smile. Jameson was already a higher member of the club when I joined. I'd heard a tale or two of him turning up at Midnight Anchor one day wearing a suit and tie, but nobody seemed to know anything about his past. He preferred it that way. But he had a naturally commanding presence and it was easy to see how he'd been welcomed into the higher ranks of the club. Over the last year or so, we'd gotten a glimpse into his previous life, and it seemed it included some pretty powerful people.

I motioned for Hope to sit and took the chair between her and Rex. Lucky perched on the side unit and Cane was sitting close to Caleb on his side of the desk. Hope had started to turn pale again, so I put my hand on her knee, hoping to calm her.

"Rex," Caleb prompted.

"Okay, here's what I was able to find out. Mickey Dolmilo was able to get his appeal heard on the basis that a law enforcement affiant provided false information in their affidavit in support of the arrest warrant. Which was impossible to prove either way as all the details regarding the case, including the warrant and affidavit, were conveniently lost."

Hope shook her head and gritted her teeth. "So, just like that they let him out."

Rex nodded. "I'm not saying the whole thing isn't fishy. It damn near reeks of corruption. But it is what it is."

"Someone at WITSEC had to have destroyed the evidence and told him where I was."

"It seems likely," Caleb added. "It also seems likely that Dolmilo knows exactly where you are now."

"Then nowhere is safe."

I squeezed Hope's knee and reached for her hand. "We'll figure this out, even if you have to be surrounded by a hundred brothers a day, we'll keep you safe until Dolmilo's stopped."

"And how long will that take?" Hope stood and paced the

small room. "How many people could get hurt because of me? What if he decides to grab someone you know to draw me out?" She gestured at Caleb. "Your wife or daughter? How can you keep everyone safe? No, I should go. I should never have put more people at risk."

Caleb's face darkened at the mention of Amber and Charlie, but he stood calmly and faced Hope. "You're not going anywhere," he said and glanced at me.

I stood and placed my hands on Hope's shoulders to stop her from pacing. "We'll figure it out," I said. "Now, sit down and trust us to work things through."

The daggers she shot me from her eyes were enough to say I'd hear about this later, and the smirk that appeared on Cane's face told me much the same. But she refrained from saying anything now and took her seat before very calmly asking what exactly we planned to do.

Rex cleared his throat. "I suggest you start with your Marshal friend, Weathers. I did a little research on him and he was retired from service three months ago."

"And how exactly will that help?" Hope asked.

Rex shrugged. "I just think it's strange that he took early retirement at the same time Dolmilo was released. If he was Dolmilo's mole inside WITSEC then it might be safe to contact them and go back into hiding. The only way we'll know for sure is if we speak to him."

I retook my chair and nodded. The thought of Hope leaving me again brought a tightness to my chest, but the important thing was to keep her alive, even if that meant she had to leave me again. Not that we were together now anyway.

"It's a place to start," I agreed. "You got a location on him?"

Rex nodded. "He's out in California, San Bernardino."

"Great," Caleb said, leaning forward in his chair. "I'll see if Amber can get you on a flight to Ontario. You can grab a hire car there."

"If they let you have one," Lucky added, smirking. "You totaled the last one you rented."

"I'm coming with you," Hope said before any of us had the chance to respond. She put her hand up when I tried to protest. "I'll go crazy if you leave me here, and I have a right to find out for myself if Weathers handed me over to Dolmilo."

Lucky chuckled and shook his head. "I think I remember an old movie with this plotline," he said. "A woman and her ex-fiancé have to find his handler when the guy he sent to prison comes after him."

"Yeah," Cane said. "Sounds great. Did everything turn out okay in the movie?"

"It's a movie. Of course, it did. Just watch out for cockroaches in the shower and stay away from zoos and tigers.

Although, if I remember correctly, it was the tigers that saved them in the end. So, if you do happen to pass a tiger pit, be sure to push Dolmilo in."

Hope smiled. "That's settled then. I'm going with Bono."

CHAPTER TWELVE

Hope

Ten hours later, after a day's rest in the spare room and not Bono's, and a hearty meal to see us through the night, we were on a flight from Denver to Ontario. It felt strange to have just traveled across the country only to be headed back west, but it was what it was. I had expected more of an argument from Bono regarding my tagging along, but as soon as I mentioned that there were no safer places than airports these days and that Dolmilo would never think I would try to reach Weathers in person, not after driving all this way in the opposite direction, he relented. Caleb had wanted to send Lucky with us too, but no-one else was keen on the idea and it was soon dropped.

By the time we'd arrived and grabbed the rental car waiting for us, I was fueled mostly on coffee and nervous anticipation. I'd always liked Weathers. He'd seemed to want to make sure I was safe and comfortable in my surroundings. He had also been the only one to sympathize with my leaving Bono behind, even if he'd never suggested I take him with me into the program. The more I thought about it, the more I doubted he would have betrayed me to Dolmilo. But the truth was, I couldn't be certain who to trust.

The sat nav directed us to an apartment complex, and a sign out front indicated a parking lot nearby. Bono followed the signs and guided the car into the lot, which was situated underneath the complex.

Bono stopped the car, reached over, and squeezed my hand. "Are you sure you want to do this?" he asked.

I scoffed. I was sure I didn't, but what choice did I have. My heart raced and my palms were sweaty. A part of me wanted Weathers to be working for Dolmilo as that may mean I could go back into hiding through WITSEC, but a bigger part of me wanted it not to be him, and not just because I liked him. If it wasn't Weathers, I'd have an excuse to spend more time with Bono.

"Do you think it's a good idea to see him it now," I asked. "I'm not sure how I'd react to someone knocking on my door a little after two in the morning."

"It's as good a time as any."

It was far too easy to enter the building and head straight up to Weathers' door on the fourth floor. I couldn't help but note the lack of security. I guess years of looking over my shoulder had me questioning everything.

My heart thundered when Bono lifted his fist and pounded on the door. "Craig Weathers. I need to talk to you," he called and knocked again. "Open the door, Sir. It's an emergency."

"Okay, okay. I'll be there in a minute," a grumpy voice called through the door. The sound of a bolt being drawn and a chain rattling followed. "Who the hell are you?" Weathers said as soon as he'd opened the door a crack.

"My name is Bono Travers. I need to talk to you about Mickey Dolmilo."

From my position behind Bono, I couldn't see Weathers' reaction, but I heard the disdain in his voice when he scoffed. "Yeah. Well, I want nothing to do with Dolmilo or anyone who associates with him."

A wave of relief washed over me at his words. Only someone who hated Dolmilo could speak about him with such venom.

"If you know what's good for you, you'll get the hell away from me," Weathers said and slammed the door.

Bono knocked again. He was about to say something when I decided it best to speak instead.

"Craig. It's me Hope Fisher," I said. "I need your help."

"Hope." The door opened a crack again. Bono stepped back. Weathers looked haggard and older than when I last saw him almost two years ago. He'd gained a fair bit of weight too and his robe didn't quite stretch around his stomach. But his eyes lit up when he saw me, and he unfastened the chain lock and ushered us both inside.

Weathers' apartment was nicer than I thought it would be given the outside. The hall area was painted an earthy green, which changed to a kind of mushroom brown in the living area. He switched on the main light and motioned for us to sit on the leather couch, pulling the gun hidden from behind his back as he did so. He didn't point the thing at us, but he didn't put it down either.

He ran his free hand over his thinning white-grey hair and pointed to the open plan kitchen. "I'm gonna need a coffee to function at this time of night," he said. "Can I get you both one?"

"Black for me, please?" Bono said.

Craig gave him a quick salute and smiled at me. "Cream and two sugars, if I remember correctly," he said.

"That would be great, thank you."

Bono sat back in the chair and pulled me back with him. "My money's on Dolmilo's mole not being your friend here," he said.

I huffed out a sigh of relief. "Mine too."

Within a few minutes, Craig had given us both our coffees and taken the chair opposite us with his own in hand. The gun, thankfully, had been left in the kitchen area. He took a sip and shook his head. "I'm glad to see you alive," he said after a moment.

"Did you have reason to think she wouldn't be?" Bono asked.

"God help me, the second I heard Dolmilo was out, I thought you were a goner."

Bono growled and sat forward, his face like thunder. "And yet you did nothing to warn her."

Craig only shook his head in response and stared wistfully into his coffee cup. "I wish that I could have. Damn well got coerced into early retirement before I could though."

"It's okay," I said. "I'm fine."

"No. It's not okay. I should have done something. I should have driven down and warned you. Tried to help, even without WITSEC."

"Then you also think someone inside has been feeding Dolmilo information."

"Oh, there's an insider alright. Do you know how many witnesses I've handled in my thirty years of service?" He raised his hand to stop us from answering. "Over two hundred. And do you know how many I've had to move because their location has been compromised? Six. And the other five were because they were stupid and tried to contact someone from their old life. You, Hope, are the only person I've had to move because Dolmilo learned where you were. I had my suspicions but couldn't prove anything. And then when all his case files went missing and it was clear he was getting out, I started setting in motion a new ID and location for you. But my boss had other ideas. He drummed up some fake charges relating to cocaine and told me to take early retirement or face prosecution. He had me packed up and out of the office before I could gather my thoughts."

"Then, it's your boss who's working for Dolmilo?" Bono said.

"I'd stake my money on it."

My head swam. If a high-up in the US Marshals was on the payroll of a mafia hitman, someone who had managed to destroy files, get Craig out of the way, and had unlimited resources at his disposal, then what hope on Earth did I have of getting out of this unscathed.

"I need to use the bathroom," I said, standing, not sure if I was about to throw up.

"Down the hall, second door on the right," Craig motioned.

"Everything okay?" Bono asked.

I hesitated mid-step and placed my arm on his, wanting nothing more than to fall against his chest and cry my heart out. Instead, I patted his arm and told him everything was fine before continuing to the bathroom.

Once inside, I stared at my reflection in the mirror for countless seconds. God, I looked old. I felt old too, even though thirty-three was anything but. I felt as though I'd lived a hundred lifetimes, and half of them in the last few days. I huffed out a breath and splashed water on my face before patting it dry and opening the door.

Craig's voice reached my ears and I hesitated. "So, you're Bono Travers," he said. "It took me a while to remember the name. You're the fiancé she had back in L.A."

"I am," Bono said.

"It damn near broke my heart the way they separated you two kids, but by the time I got involved, they'd already staged Hope's death and you'd enlisted."

"You never told Hope that."

"No. It broke her heart leaving you. The less she knew of the life you were living, the less chance there was of her contacting you. You know, there's a light in her eyes when she looks at you that I've never seen before. It's good that you kids found each other again. No matter how this turns out."

"It'll turn out with Dolmilo dead."

"I hope so."

I made a show of shutting the bathroom door loudly and heading back to the living area. Bono stood, and said it was time for us to leave.

"Thank you for your help, Craig," I said.

He pulled me in for a hug. "Take care of yourself. I don't have much of a position these days, but if there's anything I can help you with, you call, you hear?"

"Will do."

Bono shook his hand, and we left the apartment. Despite not really learning anything that could help my situation, and the overwhelming doubt that had plagued me inside, I felt strangely positive for my future.

CHAPTER THIRTEEN

Hope

We drove back to the airport and were on the first plane back to Denver. I managed to grab some sleep on the flight and only woke when Bono announced we were landing. It was a little after ten in the morning. Bono had updated his brother on his new phone before we left, and Rex along with Lucky met us at the airport.

Traffic was a nightmare, and it seemed to take forever for us to arrive back at the clubhouse. The atmosphere that greeted us when we did was chaotic and full of noise.

"Why don't you head upstairs and get some rest," Bono said. "I'll talk to Caleb and join you in a little while."

I nodded in response, too tired to wonder what he meant when he said he'd join me. When I'd made it upstairs, I decided that I had no desire to sleep alone and headed into Bono's room instead of the one I'd slept in the previous day. Or was it night? I'd lost all sense of time lately, spending my nights awake and my days asleep.

It was bright daylight outside, but thankfully, Bono had some heavy-duty blinds to block out the light, and the room plummeted into darkness as soon as I drew them. Only a faint trickle of light seeped into the room around their edges. I had a quick shower and dried myself before climbing into his bed, breathing in his musky scent, and allowing it to soothe my mind.

I stirred when a hand stroked my hair behind my ear. Half opening my eyes, I saw Bono sitting on the bed beside me. "Everything okay?" I mumbled, still half-asleep.

"Everything's fine," he answered. "I'll leave you to get some rest. There's some iced water on the table if you need a drink."

I reached out and grabbed his hand. "No. Stay. Lie with me for a while." I shifted over in the bed, and Bono stripped before climbing in beside me. Without thinking, I nestled my head beneath his chin.

"You feel so good in my arms," he whispered. "Almost like a dream."

"If this is a dream, I never want to wake up," I said and opened my eyes. Bono was smirking down at me, and I burst out laughing. "When did we get so cheesy?"

"I don't know. I think we were always a little on the cheesy side."

"Speak for yourself." I sobered and huffed out a breath. "What are we doing?" I asked after a moment.

"I haven't got a fucking clue."

"Do you… do you think it's a bad idea us to be here together, naked in your bed?" I asked the question unsure if I wanted the answer.

"Do you?" He trailed his hand down to the small of my back and pulled me tight against his body. The rigid outline of his erection pressed against my stomach, and I moaned.

"At least one part of you is happy to see me," I said.

"Why would you say that?" he asked. "How could you not know how every fiber of my being has been crying out for you since the day I thought you died? I missed you so much."

"Are we bordering on cheesy again?" I asked in an attempt to make the tension between us something more manageable.

My whole body tingled, and goosebumps rose on my skin when he brushed his lips against the pulse point on my neck.

"Why are you doing that?" he asked, trailing a line of soft, teasing kisses along my collarbone. "Why are you keeping your distance, pushing me away?"

"We're in bed together. I wouldn't call that pushing you away."

He continued his path down my body, kissing and licking with agonizing gentleness, cupping my breast in his hand.

"That's not what I meant, and you know it," he said and rolled my nipple between his fingers before taking it in his mouth, swirling and flicking his tongue over the hard bud.

"I can't lose you again," I said, shocked to feel a tear run down my cheek.

"You never lost me." He suckled hard while his hand slid between my thighs and into my panties. He circled my clit with slow, relentless pressure. Bolts of pleasure shot directly to my core. Bono removed his mouth from my breast and claimed my lips. "I've always been yours."

"I want you to fuck me," I gasped, reaching for his cock.

"Is that a fact?"

"Yes."

"I will."

I laughed. "A gentleman should never keep a lady waiting."

Bono smiled and nipped at my bottom lip. "Whoever said I was a gentleman?" He flipped me on my back and snagged my panties, tugging them down my legs and tossing them into the dark room.

He trailed his cock down my body, making me itch to grab it and guide it where it needed to be. Before I could, he snatched hold of my knees, pushed my legs apart, and teased at my entrance with its tip. My legs quivered, and I pushed upward, wanting to feel him inside me.

"You always were impatient," he said and flicked my clit with his finger.

I moaned and reached down to grab him and push him inside. He grabbed my hand and pushed it above my head, holding it in place, while he continued his relentless teasing. I so fucking needed to feel him inside me. I wriggled my body, driving his cock against my wet core and over my clit. He pushed inside slowly, filling me up inch by inch. Deliciously stretching me. He was long, and thick, and more than I could ever hope for. I cried out in pure joy.

"Fuck your pussy is perfect. But I want to fuck every part of you," he said, pushing into me in swift, hard strokes, over and over. "Tight and wet and needy. I need to fucking taste you."

"No, Bono," I cried out when he left me. "I need…"

Bono chuckled. "Don't worry, you'll get what you need." He leaned over me, his eyes claiming every part of my body. After what felt like an eternity, he lowered his head between my legs. He licked my slit up and down as I seeped for him. His tongue circled my clit, flicking and teasing, as he pushed his fingers inside me one at a time. His tongue and fingers were relentless, pushing me higher and higher.

Everything about this felt so good. I was Bono's and Bono was mine. I moaned and closed my eyes, my body panting and shaking, enjoying the sensation of being one with Bono.

Pleasure sparked. My core clenched, wanting more.

"Oh, fuck… Bono." My whole body lit up and flashes of light sparked behind my eyelids. Pleasure swamped my body. I thought I'd blackout from the sensations swirling through me.

He was so fucking perfect. I could come over and over again just thinking of him watching me get off. As soon as I recovered from my orgasm, I knew I had to taste him. "You wanted to fuck every part of me," I said before pushing him back.

I climbed over him, pushing my ass out into the air, and trailed my hands down his chest and over his arms, tracing his tattoos. Using one hand for support, I cupped his balls and kneaded them with my hands before zeroing in on his cock and licking the precum from his slit.

Fuck! He tasted too fucking good.

His hands circled in my hair as I took him slowly into my wet, warm mouth. He thrust his hips, pushing in deeper. I let out a gasping moan, hoping desperately that he'd fuck my mouth the way he promised.

His head flung back, and he groaned as the head of his cock brushed against the back of my throat. He pulled my head downward, just as I wanted, thrusting his hips, and shoving his cock deeper and deeper.

I closed my eyes, relishing the sensation of him moving within me. His cock trembled inside my mouth. He growled and pushed me off, shoving me back down onto the bed.

I felt like I was on fire when he spread my legs wide and pushed his cock inside me with one hard thrust as deep as he could go.

I arched against him and ran my hands over his chest and relished the way his muscles shifted under my fingertips, working hard to ensure his thick, long cock gave me maximum pleasure.

"Fuck me like you promised," I said between whimpers. "Harder, deeper."

Bono ran kisses by the side of my ear, and his lips down my neck, tickling me with his facial hair. I hadn't been sure how I felt about the way it looked at first, but the tingling sensations it created along my skin had my heart skipping a beat.

Bono withdrew, slipped me on my front, and wrapped his arm around my waist from behind, pulling my ass into the air against him. He ran his hand over the curve of my bottom and teased at my entrance with his fingers. I moaned, and pushed back into them, wanting more. Wanting to feel his cock inside me again.

"Do you remember that time in Santa Monica?" he asked.

A pang of nervous excitement washed over my body. "We don't have any ice."

"Yes, we do."

My eyes darted to the glass, forgotten on the bedside table. It was more ice than water, even though a large portion of it had melted. Bono removed his fingers from my core and grabbed a chunk of ice from the glass. He circled it around my clit, making me jerk away from the extreme cold. Chills rushed up my back and goosebumps flared on my legs.

He teased me, running the ice cube over my bottom and the backs of my thighs until it melted. Then, reaching into the drawer on the bedside table, he produced a condom, which he proceeded to fill with two pieces of the ice remaining in the glass. I shuddered when he pressed it to my entrance.

"Please," I murmured.

He pushed it inside. My core clenched tight around it. Bono swiped a decisive tongue up my folds and grazed my clit. I whimpered, the hot touch of his breath a stark contrast to the cold ice pressed inside me. Liquid dripped down my leg. A gasp fell from my lips as he sucked on my clit. His tongue circled the bundle of nerves without mercy. I squirmed, desperate for more. He pressed two fingers inside with the ice, rolling it around, and brushing right against my G-spot. My orgasm built, coiling inside me. I screamed out as it exploded, washing over me in waves.

Bono pulled out the condom and pushed the tip of his cock into my entrance. "Fuck," he said. "The ice has made you so fucking tight."

He pushed me down onto my belly and straddled his legs either side of mine before thrusting firmly inside me. I cried out. He felt so fucking big, I felt sure I would burst as he slammed into me over and over. He grabbed my hand and pushed it between my legs. I flicked and pinched my clit, teasing it as Bono pummeled into me.

I couldn't hold back the cries of pleasure as another orgasm crashed through my body.

"I'm gonna make you come all fucking day," Bono said.

I smiled. "We do have a lot of time to make up for."

CHAPTER FOURTEEN

Bono

It was near ten at night when we woke, and hunger drove us from the room. Hope was reluctant to leave, but I assured her the rooms were sound-proofed and no one would know what went on inside. We'd managed to grab some coffee as well as more eggs and bacon before Cane found us in the kitchen.

"Jameson called," he said. "Caleb wants us in his office."

Hope sighed and I knew she'd wanted to pretend the outside world didn't exist for a while longer. I did too. I offered her another cup of coffee, which she refused, and we headed to the office. Only Cane and Caleb were there.

"What did Jameson have to say?" I asked as soon as we'd taken our seats.

"He can tell you himself," Caleb answered.

"Dolmilo's on his own." Jameson's voice came through on the speakerphone. "The mafia families have agreed to lend him no support in his quest against Hope, and that there will be no retaliatory action should he turn up dead."

"How the fuck did you manage that?" Cane asked.

"Let's just say, I called in a favor or two and owe a few more."

"I don't understand what this means," Hope said, shaking her head.

I clasped onto her hand. "It means that after we kill the fucker all this will be over." She shifted uncomfortably in her seat. I knew the thought of killing anyone disgusted her. We'd both seen far too many lives ended prematurely. "Don't think of it as murder," I said. "Think of it as justice."

"Vigilante justice," she said.

"Maybe, maybe not," Cane said while pulling a face that told me he was thinking something through. He'd killed to protect Thea. First when a fucker attempted to rape her, and then her stepbrother, who was trying to kill Thea at the time.

"Dolmilo wouldn't hesitate to kill any one of us, and you're at the top of that list," Caleb added. "We would never set out to murder someone, but we will protect our own."

"But I'm not one of your own."

Caleb glanced from Hope to me and back again. "That's for you and Bono to decide," he said. "But either way, you currently fall under our protection." He added a smile at the end of his words. "Think of it as feeding our hero complex as Amber called it."

Hope smiled back and sighed before shaking her head. "You still have to find him before he finds me or tries to hurt someone else to get to me."

"Where's Thea and the baby?" I asked, realizing that she had to now be out of the hospital.

Cane clapped me on the shoulder. "They're both at Caleb's with Amber, Charlie, and a few brothers to keep them safe."

"This isn't right," Hope said after clearing her throat. "You have families. A new baby. You should be with them, not worrying over me. This could go on way too long."

Cane smiled. "Caleb has a plan."

Hope's eyes darted to Caleb, but from the look on his face, I knew exactly what his plan was.

"We are not using Hope as fucking bait," I said, standing. My anger flared at even the thought. "A million fucking things could go wrong."

Hope remained quiet while Cane and Caleb both tried to talk me around. The fuckers would never have considered the action if it was Thea or Amber on the line. In fact, they did everything they could to keep them safe, and not send them out into danger. Fuck! Cane was so protective over Thea, even after he'd agreed to let her return to work at Forever Midnight, he always followed her and stayed outside on his bike to make sure she was okay.

"Let's do it," Hope said, silencing us all. "How will it work?

Should I just go to a motel or something?"

"No. It's ridiculous to even consider this. It's not gonna happen. What about using Lucky in a wig, the same way we did when protecting Amber?" I asked.

"Dolmilo's too smart to fall for that," Jameson said over the line, reminding me he was still there.

Hope grabbed my hand and pulled it to her chest. "I'm going to do this." The look in her eyes told me there was no room for argument. Either she did it with my help, or she'd do it without me.

I growled and ran my hand over my head before taking my seat again. "I will make you fucking pay if anything happens to her," I told Caleb.

His neck strained as the pulse in his head twitched. He looked like he was about to bite my head off, but Cane interjected. "Nothing's going to happen. We just have to figure out the details and set everything in motion."

~

It was late the next afternoon when I drove with Hope towards the same safe house we'd used to hide Amber. Only, instead of hiding Hope there, the plan was to make her far too visible. Jameson had decided it the best place to lay the trap and wait. Knowing the lay of the land, I'd have preferred my cabin, but he thought Dolmilo would find that suspicious given the fact he knew that we knew that he knew about me, or some other such confusing shit.

"Are you sure I can't talk you out of this?" I asked as I stopped the jeep and glanced around the grounds that surrounded the house. There were far too many places for Dolmilo to hide, but that also meant there were a lot of areas for my brothers to conceal themselves too.

"It's for the best," Hope said. "I just want everything over with one way or another."

I reached over and grabbed her hand, giving it a reassuring squeeze. "I'm not gonna let anything happen to you."

She brushed the back of her hand over my cheek. "I know. Now, let's join the others. I'd feel a lot better about this if I knew everything involved."

Caleb had trucked in a contingent of brothers to ensure no motorbikes were seen around the property. He and Cane were talking to them. I grabbed hold of Hope's hand and set off toward them.

My boots squelched on the muddy ground. I glanced at the sky and noted the heavy, black clouds gathering overhead. We were in for a soaking. I steadied my breathing and pushed down the growing sense of dread that built in my stomach.

Caleb nodded past me back at the house. "Lucky and Rex

are gonna be inside with Hope," he said. "They'll keep to the top floor unless they need to come down. The rest of the brothers will be staged in a few spots around the house under the cover of the trees. There's also a small outbuilding that gives a good view of both the road and the house. You, Cane, and I can keep a watch from there."

After a few minutes of discussion where he outlined the plan, I shook my head. They were putting far too much reliance on Dolmilo taking the bait, and on us spotting him.

"I'm staying with Hope in the house," I said.

Caleb shared a look with Cane before shaking his head. "Dolmilo needs to think you're out of the picture."

"I see no sense in that."

Cane patted me on the back. "You're an ex-marine," he said. "Dolmilo will know that. It's better if he thinks that you're not here. Besides, we don't plan on him getting anywhere near the house. You can ensure that yourself by taking your watch outside."

"It makes sense," Hope said, still holding tightly to my hand.

I grumbled and shook my head, dragging her away. "We're out of here. This is a dumb fucking idea."

"Weathers is going for it," Rex said, jogging up to join us, and halting our tracks. "I have the contact details for the insider at WITSEC, he believes is working for Dolmilo."

"See," Hope said, pulling me to a stop. "This is going to work. We just have to play our parts."

My nostrils flared. I sucked in a deep breath and looked into her eyes. "When do we get the ball rolling?" I asked, relenting.

Cane glanced at the sky. "We're all gonna get fucking wet, but we're in place for tonight."

CHAPTER FIFTEEN

Bono

Rex handed out comms units and Caleb gave guns to those not already carrying. I made my way to the house with Hope.

"It's not too late to back out," I said once we were alone in the sitting room, even though I knew I was wasting my breath.

She gathered her arms around me and leaned her head against my chest. "I've been on the run for ten years," she said. "I'm done waiting to get my life back."

"I can't lose you again." I kissed her forehead and pulled her close, inhaling her scent.

"You never lost me," she said, echoing my earlier words. "I've always been yours."

Rex barged into the room, carrying a phone and his laptop. He cleared his throat when he saw us and moved to leave.

"It's okay," Hope said, pulling away from me. "Is everything ready?"

Rex glanced from Hope to me and back again. "Yeah, we're good to go."

Hope nodded and reached for the phone along with the piece of paper with Weathers's' ex-boss's number on it.

She paced the room while dialing the number. We listened to it ring on speaker, waiting with bated breath for someone to answer.

"Hello," Hope said as soon as a male voice answered. "I need to speak with Craig Weathers. It's a matter of urgency."

She perched on the edge of the couch, rubbing her forehead with a trembling hand, and waited for the other person to speak. I sat next to her and pulled her tight against me.

"Who is this?" the man asked.

"I really can't say. Could you just put me through to Craig Weathers, please? I can't reach him on his number. The line seems disconnected," she added, something Rex had confirmed of the contact number Hope had for him. "I had this one in case of emergencies."

"I'm sorry to tell you this, but Special Agent Weathers is no longer with us."

Hope let out a gasping sob and real tears streamed down her cheeks. "Then what do I do?" she asked.

"Tell me your situation and I'll help," the man said.

"I shouldn't talk to anyone but Craig." She sobbed again. "He wouldn't leave without telling me. Who are you?"

"My name is Special Agent Peter Munfry," he said, confirming he was the man we needed to speak to. "I worked with Craig, and I can help you. You just need to tell me who you are and the situation you're in."

Hope remained silent along the line for a moment, and I wondered if she was having second thoughts.

"Ma'am," Munfry continued. "I can help you."

Hope let out a deep breath. "This is Hope Fisher," she said. "ID code, TL9236480. My position was compromised, and Mickey Dolmilo has tried to kill me."

The rest of the conversation comprised of Hope giving Munfry details of what happened when she saw Dolmilo at the bar and later when we were run off the road. She also confirmed her exact location. "There's one more thing," she said when Munrfy told her to stay put and that he'd have someone out to her within twelve hours. "I reached out to someone from my old life, my fiancé, Bono Travers. I need him to come with me."

"That's not going to be possible," Munfry said.

Hope sniffed back tears. "You have to make it happen. Dolmilo tried to kill him too."

Munfry huffed down the line, impatient. "He wasn't part of the initial deal," he said. "I'll see what I can do, but you might have to leave him behind."

"If that's the case, then you need to come sooner," Hope said. She cleared her throat before speaking but her voice still broke on the words. "He's heading back to Castel Rock in the next hour to sort a few things out. He'll be back first thing in the morning. If I'm not gone by then. I just… I just don't know what to do. If Bono can't come with me, you have to come for me while I'm alone."

"Everything's going to be fine," Munfry said. "I'll come myself. Just stay put and don't panic. We'll have you set up with a new identity in no time."

"How will I know that it's you?" Hope asked.

"I'll have ID. I also have a slight limp in my left leg. An old injury. It's the reason, I usually stay behind a desk instead of venturing into the field."

"Thank you," Hope said and hung up.

Rex punched some keys on his laptop to end the recording. "Got it. Weathers is gonna love it." He shook his head and chuckled. "That was one hell of a performance. You should be a fucking actress."

I looked at Hope and she gave me a tight smile. We both knew she hadn't been acting. "I'm going to be right outside," I said. "Dolmilo's not going to get within an inch of this house."

Hope sucked on her lip and nodded her head. Rex excused himself, saying he had to check everything was set around the house, and left, but not before giving Hope a comms unit and showing her how to use it.

"You look tired," she said and stroked my face again. "We should have gotten more rest."

"We'll rest when this is over," I promised, knowing I wouldn't be able to sleep until this matter was settled. "I've got to go. Talk to me over the comms, so I know you're alright, okay?" Hope nodded and we stood. "Rex said that this house has a state-of-the-art security system. He's going to put it on as soon as I leave. No one's getting in here without every brother in the area knowing about it. Stay away from the doors and windows. There's a crawl space at the back of the walk-in closet in the master bedroom. Rex said it's a good place to hide."

"I don't want to hide." I nodded and turned to leave. Hope pulled me back and kissed me hard on the lips. "But I do want a gun," she said when she pulled back.

I pulled the gun Caleb had handed me from the belt of my pants. "Do you know how to use this?" I asked.

Hope smiled and took it from me. With practiced hands, she checked the barrel and chamber. "I've been to the range every weekend for over eight years. I know how to use it," she said.

I pulled her in for another kiss. "That's my girl," I said, feeling a damn sight better about using her as bait, knowing she had the means to defend herself. "Is there anything else I should know?" I asked.

"Only that I have a black-belt in jiu-jitsu, I guess."

I shook my head and laughed.

CHAPTER SIXTEEN

Bono

I pulled away from the house in my jeep, wishing for all the world Hope was in it with me and we could ride away into the sunset. After I'd gone a fair distance, I pulled off the road and into a field out of sight and made my way on foot to the outbuilding where I was set to keep watch with Cane and Caleb.

A light drizzle had started by the time I arrived. "I'm with the others now, Hope," I said into my comms unit.

"Okay. The waiting is driving me crazy. Do you think it would be alright for me to go lie down?"

"Yeah, of course. I'll speak to you in a little while. Keep your comms unit on, okay?"

"Will do." I switched mine off and sat against the wall next to Caleb when Cane said he'd keep watch. If I didn't think it too early for anything to happen, I'd have refused his offer and kept my eyes glued to the house and the road.

"Anything to report?" Caleb said into his comms unit.

"Position one, nothing to report," one of my brothers answered.

"Position two. Likewise."

"Same for position three."

"Nothing to report at the house, either," Rex added.

"Okay, keep me updated if you see anything," Caleb said and switched off his mic. "How you holding up?" he asked me.

I chuckled and rested my head against the wall. "I've had better days."

He nodded. "You and Hope seem to be hitting it off. After all this is over, do you think she'll stick around?" He cleared his throat. "Do you want her to?"

"I haven't got a fucking clue what either of us wants," I said, and Caleb smiled. I sat forward and looked at him. "I don't know how the fuck you did it with Amber."

"What do you mean?" he asked.

"It's just... I'm glad Hope's alive, and damn it, I still fucking love her. But so much has happened in both our lives. How did you just put all that behind you and move on?"

This time it was Caleb who leaned his head against the wall and sighed. "During all the shit with Leo, all I could think about was keeping her safe and having her near me again. I didn't take the time then to think things through. I acted on instinct."

"And now?" I asked, picking up on the word 'then'.

"I love Amber and Charlie, but I'd be lying if I said there weren't times when I hate that she left the way she did, that I missed so much of Charlie's life, of both their lives because she chose to run away instead of talking to me. But I have to accept that's what happened, because it did, and I can't change it, and I need to keep them both in my life."

I looked at the president of Forever Midnight MC and realized that was the most he'd ever confided in me about his personal life. It was easy to forget how much crap everyone else had been through when wallowing in my own.

"And that's what you both have to do," he added. "If you want to be together now, if you love each other, then you have to accept the past and move on, together." He rubbed at his eyes. "Amber still pushes me to get a paternity test every now and then," he added out of the blue.

"Do you think you'll do it?" Cane asked from his position by the door.

Caleb shrugged. "Right now, Charlie's my daughter. Of that I'm certain, and so is Amber. It's why she wants me to take the test."

"So, what's the problem?" I asked.

Caleb looked me in the eyes. "What if we're wrong?"

"Would it make a difference?"

"Not to me, and I doubt it would to Amber. But what about

Charlie? What happens if at some point in the future, we slip up and she discovers Leo was her biological father and she was a product of rape? How would that make her feel?"

"Life's a big fucking ball of shit ninety-nine percent of the time," I said not knowing how to solve any of our problems.

"Not anymore." Caleb shook his head. "Not with Amber and Charlie in my life. And not with Thea and the baby, right Cane?"

"Fucking right." Cane smiled at me, and Caleb laughed.

"See. I didn't even know his mouth could make that hideous shape he calls a smile. I have no idea what Thea sees in that ugly fucker."

"I take after my brother," Cane said, and we all laughed.

~

Six hours passed. Everyone was restless. I resisted growling out my frustration. This had never been a good plan to start with and it was pretty clear it had failed. Hell, we were all probably wrong about Munfry, and he'd turn up in the morning ready to take Hope and me into protective custody. We'd all face a shitstorm then.

The rain worsened, opening up the heavens with a torrential downpour.

"Fuck. It's practically biblical," Cane said, glancing over my shoulder as I crouched by the doorway, taking my turn to watch.

To punctuate his words, one of the brothers called through the comms, shouting to be heard above the wind and the rain. "Our position isn't sustainable," he said. "Back-up's getting restless and wondering if this is all a waste of time and resources."

"We're experiencing the same problem," a second brother added.

"Fuck! He should have been here by now," Cane said, but my ears were focused on another sound. A faint rumble just audible beneath the thundering rain.

I turned my attention to the road. A gleam of headlights came into view. From the angle, and height, I guessed the vehicle to be a van. I nudged Cane and he motioned Caleb over. After a brief moment, the lights disappeared and the rumble of the engine cut.

"Get ready to act," Caleb said into his comms unit. "We might have something here, brothers."

"Hope," I called through mine.

"I'm here," she answered, and a lump formed in my throat.

"We need to move closer," I said, glancing at my brothers.

Cane and Caleb agreed. We started to move, but another vehicle came up the road and turned into the driveway of the house. It surprised us all and drove right up to the building. Some fucker in a suit got out of the car, opened an umbrella over his head, and limped toward the house.

"Munfry," I said, remembering he'd mentioned his limp.

"You think he's here to move Hope?" Cane asked.

I squinted into the distance. It was a possibility, but what about the van that arrived moments before him. I shook my head. "I don't like it."

"Me neither," Caleb added.

The lights were on in the house, illuminating the area with a dappled glow through the falling rain. A low growl built in my chest as I watched Munfry climb the steps to the front door and knock. I clenched my fists and listened to the voice inside my head that told me everything about this situation was wrong. He glanced back along the drive in the direction of where I knew the first car had stopped.

"Do you think he's here to deal with Hope himself?" Cane asked.

"No," I answered. "He's making a fucking distraction. Everyone, get to the fucking house. Hope, don't answer the door," I called into the comms, sure that we'd made the biggest fucking mistake of our lives.

I sprang to my feet as a gang of men edged around the outbuilding. I ducked back inside, hoping they hadn't seen me and that the rain had covered my voice.

From the brief glimpse I'd caught, there were three of

them, stocky men, wearing black waterproofs overlaid with stab jackets. They slunk around the side of the building. I motioned with my finger for Caleb and Cane to keep quiet. I held my breath and pushed up against the wall next to the door. I felt more than heard them do the same on the outside. Nothing happened for several seconds, but then, the door nudged open. Still none of us moved until the barrel of a Heckler & Koch MP5 submachine gun emerged through the gap.

I didn't hesitate in moving. I grabbed the barrel of the gun, squeezing my finger behind the trigger to stop it from firing; yanked its owner into the room; and slammed the weapon into his face.

CHAPTER SEVENTEEN

Hope

The rain pounded and the wind lashed tree branches against the window. My heart dropped into my stomach as I tried to block out the sound of Munfry thumping on the door from outside.

"Hope, it's Special Agent Peter Munfry," he called.

I stood in the doorway of the living room just out of sight. Rex perched on the stairs, and Lucky hung back around the corner of the kitchen doorway. Rex pressed a finger to his mouth telling me to keep quiet.

In the shadows outside, we noted Munfry pulling what looked like a gun. Rex motioned for me to come to him. I glanced at the dark stained-glass windows on the front door worried that Munrfy would spot my movement as surely as I saw him and hesitated. Only when it looked as though his back was turned did I move.

The first step on the stairs creaked when I stepped on it and

I froze. Munfry's voice sounded outside, muffled and indistinct. It was clear he wasn't calling into the house when I caught the words, "I'm going in." I couldn't hear the response that followed, but Munfry said, "Okay, two minutes. Count me down when you're ready."

I rushed up the next step, and quickly told Rex what I'd heard. He nodded and motioned me up the stairs and into the master bedroom.

I went, but although my heart raced and my legs felt like they would crumble beneath me, I refused to climb in the wardrobe hidey-hole. Instead, I pulled the gun and waited by the door, never in my life as possessed by fear the way I was then. Not when Kate had been murdered and I hid from Dolmilo under the desk, not knowing if he'd find me and kill me next, and not when I'd run scared and alone through the streets, hiding out in bars. I realized then that my fear was no longer just for me. It was for the man I loved.

"Bono," I said, speaking into my comms unit, wanting to feel less alone and to know he was safe. My mouth dried and my stomach lurched when he didn't respond.

The house moaned and creaked around me, making my skin crawl. The two minutes Munfry had mentioned seemed more like twenty, but eventually, a gunshot sounded, and the front door blasted open with a reverberating crash as it smashed against the wall and the stained-glass window shattered.

The whole house lit up with every light coming on and an alarm blaring. Rex shouted. Lucky followed suit. More gunshots, and the thud of people fighting.

My skin crawled. Despite the commotion downstairs, I couldn't shake the feeling that upstairs, I was no longer alone, that the crash of the front door smashing against the wall wasn't the only source of breaking glass I'd heard.

Warning bells screamed in my head. "Bono," I said again into the comms.

"Hope," he answered, making my heart soar. "SWAT is here. They've caught three men. Do Rex and Lucky have Munfry?"

"We've got him pinned," Rex answered in my stead.

"Great. Stay put. I'm coming to you."

I stepped into the hall, holding my gun out in front of me ready to fire at any movement. But as I rounded the bend toward the top of the stairs, I was unprepared for the blow that smashed down onto my hands. I lost the gun in a flash but managed to duck a second blow aimed at my head.

Dolmilo drove forward like a battering ram. I lashed out, trying to take him down, but flinched back when a blade sliced my arm. Dolmilo backhanded me, making my cheek sting and my eyes water. The next moment, I was pinned against the wall with a knife to my throat, every shred of martial arts training forgotten. It was far different facing someone who wanted to kill me than it was a sparring partner.

He pressed the knife tight against my skin, stealing my breath. "You have been so much fucking trouble. I should kill you now and be done with it."

I stared deep into his eyes and fought my fear. "Just do it," I said.

He laughed. "Don't fucking tempt me." Instead, he snatched the comms unit from me and spoke into the mic. "I have your woman," he said. "If you have any hope of seeing her alive, you'll pull everyone back away from the house."

"If you hurt one hair on her head, I will fucking kill you," Bono's voice sounded cold along the open channel.

"Yeah. You think you and your fucking army of brothers are better than me? I got past you all and into the house without you seeing. You really think I can't get out and take you down one by one?"

I could barely breathe, but I had to get the panic flooding me under control. There was no doubt in my mind that Dolmilo would use me as a shield to escape and then kill me as he'd always intended.

He grabbed my hair and flipped me around to face the stairs. With the knife still to my throat, he released my hair and pulled a gun, holding it in his other hand as he wrapped his arm around my waist. I flinched as the movement caused the knife to dig deeper into my flesh, knowing that a fraction of an inch more would see me dead.

My mind ran through a number of possibilities. In training, I'd grab his knife arm and twist until I had it behind his back. But that didn't take into account the gun, and in practice the fake blade had never had the tip pressed tightly against my jugular so that even swallowing caused it to press deeper into my skin.

We stood at the top step. The alarm bells still blaring, making it hard to think. In the hallway below, Rex and Lucky were nowhere to be seen.

"In the kitchen, both of you," Dolmilo called into the empty space.

After a moment, Rex appeared in the open front doorway. He chucked his gun on the floor and raised his arms above his head. Lucky stepped forward still holding Munrfy, whose hands were pinned behind his back. He pushed him, making him stumble forward. While he recovered, Lucky tossed his gun to join Rex's, raised his hands, and stepped through the doorway behind Rex.

"Kitchen now," Dolmilo said and nudged me in the back, making me slowly step down the stairs, one at a time, always careful to keep fully between him and the men below.

Rex and Lucky never took their eyes off us. "It's gonna be

fine, Hope," Lucky said.

Munfry dusted himself off in the front doorway before bending down and picking up one of the guns. He leveled it at Bono's brothers. I closed my eyes. Dolmilo released his grip on me for a fraction of a second and a shot rang out. My ears screamed a constant eeeEEEEeeeEEEE. I wanted to cover them and bury my head in my hands from the shock.

I opened my eyes to see Munfry, staring at us wide-eyed, while clutching his stomach. He fell to the floor. His usefulness to Dolmilo was over.

Dolmilo whipped his arm around my waist and whirled me to face Rex and Lucky. He flicked the knife up. I cried out as the sharp blade sliced my chin. Unable to stop the movement of my hand, it flew to the gash and came away bloody. I could do nothing but stare at the blood dripping from my fingers.

"Get in the fucking kitchen and close the door, now," Dolmilo yelled, above the ringing in my ears. "If I see even one person near the house, I'll slice her from ear to ear. You got that?" he screamed.

"We understand," Caleb's voice sounded through the comms as the kitchen door clicked shut, sealing Rex and Lucky away from view.

I was too busy moving robotically down the stairs at Dolmilo's bidding and staring at the blood on my hands, wondering how much blood Dolmilo had on his. I knew about Kate. The Marshals told me that she'd got involved with the wrong people and a hit had been put on her head. Dolmilo went to prison because I saw him, but the person who hired him was never brought to justice. Nor the full reason for her murder brought to light. He'd also shot Munfry not moments before, but how many more people were there. As a hitman for the mafia there had to be too many to even comprehend. He had no compassion. He didn't care about anyone or anything. And now, as small an amount as it was, he'd spilled my blood. Not once — I glanced to the blood on my fingers from under my chin — but twice — my gaze shifted to the nick on my arm.

As I stepped through the open front door and Dolmilo guided me toward Munfry's car, waiting outside, I realized for the first time that I no longer felt fear. Instead, an anger that had been building inside me for ten years grew like a fire in my belly and erupted to the surface.

I screamed and grabbed the wrist holding the knife to my throat while driving my shoulder up and the blade down. I slid down and rotated toward him, keeping the motion going until he had no choice but to release the knife. In the split second he did so, I threw it to the ground and kicked the gun out of his other hand. I followed through with a punch to the nose.

Instead of going down, the bastard laughed and wiped away

the blood dripping onto his upper lip. His fist slammed into my face, and I fell to the ground, my vision a haze that matched the ringing in my ears. Everything swirled in a maelstrom of chaos.

CHAPTER EIGHTEEN

Bono

Hearing Dolmilo threaten Hope through the comms had set my blood boiling. It didn't matter that SWAT teams were in place around the building, that we'd worked so carefully with Weathers to see him brought down. I wanted to rip his head off.

Cane had come up with the plan when Hope had called the trap for Dolmilo 'vigilante justice'. He said the note in her voice told him she would never look at me the same way if I killed him myself.

We'd been so careful with everything, even though I'd never liked the idea, and Weathers was all too willing to help. Rex had sent the recording of Hope's phone call to Peter Munfry to him within seconds of making it. He'd been waiting in the office of the Head of Special Agents. As soon as they had the recording, they found that Munrfy had immediately processed a request for personal leave, but never processed a single document relating to Hope. From there it was easy enough to get a warrant and a team in place around the house to see if Dolmilo showed up, adding weight to the case against Munfry. Of course, Munfry turning up as well had thrown all sets of questions up in the air. Only the capture of three men stalking the house had kept SWAT on our side.

But all that meant nothing with Hope at Dolmilo's mercy. Everyone else had pulled back at his command, but there was no fucking way I would let him leave with her. Not a person amongst us believed he would keep her alive the second he thought he was safe to kill her.

I crawled through the clawing mud toward the house, trying to still the worry making the blood thump in my ears. The rain stopped, and I watched Rex and Lucky drag Munfry outside. Lucky had him pinned to the wall.

When the shot rang out after they went back inside with their hands raised, I'd almost given up my steady crawl and charged, risking everything to reach Hope and them. But when Munfry fell, a well of relief filled my chest, and I continued my hidden approach. I'd reached Munfry's car by the time Dolmilo threatened to cut Hope from ear to ear.

Time slowed and my heart almost stopped when Dolmilo came out of the house with Hope in his arms, a knife to her throat, and a gun in her stomach. Blood dripping from her hand.

I willed a SWAT marksman to take him out, instead, Hope made her move, and so did I.

As I charged toward them, my mind played over every fucking moment of loss. Falling to the ground, a lifetime ago, when the cops knocked on my door and told me Hope was dead, standing over her grave and seeing the coffin lowered into the ground. My heart broke all over again. Then I saw Tony, all too trusting, approaching a child, crying in the street. I didn't get the chance to utter a word of warning before an explosion ripped through the world in a blaze of color and wiped them from the Earth. Too many times, I had seen people I cared about suffer and die, and all that had started with what Dolmilo had done.

I reached them a second too late to stop the blow that landed on Hope's face and had her battling to stay conscious on the ground, but not too late to stop Dolmilo from picking up the knife he'd used to hurt her.

The expression on his face changed from one of pride in her suffering to one of fear when he registered my presence. He dodged my first blow, but I wasn't going to wait around for him to gather his wits and retaliate. I landed a punch to his stomach and then a kick to his groin.

From the corner of my eye, I saw Hope roll on her front and crawl a few steps forward. *That's it,* I thought. *Get as far from him as possible.*

My moment's distraction gave Dolmilo the chance to recover. He came at me, landing a right hook to my gut that damn near knocked the wind from me. But I wasn't going down easy. I stepped into his next blow, dodged to the side, and grabbed his overextended arm, pulling him further forward. Stepping into him, I turned my back to land a reverse punch to his face. Then, I used his weight against him with a hip throw, which had him on the ground scrambling to get up.

He rose with the knife in his hands. He feinted left but sprinted right and toward Hope. A guttural roar ripped through me when he grabbed her arm and pulled her to her feet, swinging the knife in a forward motion towards her stomach.

A gunshot boomed through the air. Hope and Dolmilo both fell to the ground. I rushed toward them as my brothers and the SWAT team surrounded us.

"Hope," I said, brushing her hair from her face with my muddy hand.

She spluttered and pulled her hand away from her side. It was covered in blood. "We need an ambulance," I shouted while applying pressure to her wound.

She smiled and reached up to touch my face. "I slayed my demons," she said and made a strange choking sound, I thought might be laughter.

I glanced at Dolmilo. The back of his head had been blasted

away by the gun that still rested in Hope's other hand. "Yeah, you did. That's my girl. My Hope."

"My Bono," she said and smiled.

Cane landed on the ground beside me, and I told him to raise her legs to help with the shock. I glanced at my hands, beneath the pressure I could see the bleeding was slowing, but not quickly enough.

"Stay with me, Hope. You're going to be fine." I said the words knowing she had to be, I couldn't lose her again. She blinked up at me, and her eyes glazed over and rolled into her head. "Stay with me Hope."

EPILOGUE

(Sixteen Hours Later)

Hope

Everything hurt when I awoke. I lay still, keeping my eyes shut tight, and listened to the bleep of machinery. I found it comforting, knowing that the sound represented my heart beating and that it was going strong.

I shifted my focus to the senseless chatter of faraway voices and sensed the presence of a person in the room. They moved closer and a hand entwined with my own. I knew it had to be Bono when he lifted my hand to his mouth and gave it a gentle kiss.

"Good morning," I said, and opened my eyes.

Bono's caring, dark eyes met mine and he smiled. "Good afternoon," he said and shifted closer. "How are you feeling today?"

"Everything still hurts, but I don't feel as weak as I did when they brought me in."

"Time and rest will do what the medicine and doctors kickstarted." His face dropped and he shut his eyes for a moment, the strain on his face evident.

"Did you manage any sleep?" I asked.

"Not much," he confessed.

"Hey," I said, shaking and squeezing his hand. "Why so glum? I'm fine just like you promised I'd be."

"No thanks to me."

I shook my head and brushed my hand against the fluff of his beard. "All thanks to you." He huffed out a breath and I knew it would be a while before he accepted that he wasn't to blame for my predicament. "When did the doctor say I could leave?" I asked.

"She wants to keep you in one more night."

I rolled my eyes back into my head. "Ugh, can't they discharge me already, I'm not that bad?"

"Hope, as well as a nasty gash in the side, you have two broken ribs. Why don't you do as the doctor says and rest up?"

"Fine, but only if you sneak me in some food. I'm starving."

Bono laughed. "That I can do." A knock sounded on the door, and Bono turned to the noise. "There are a few people who want to check in and see that you're okay," he said while motioning them inside.

"Hey, Charlie," I said as she ran up to my bed.

"Now you look like you've been in a car accident," she said, and Amber told her not to be rude while Caleb came up behind her and rested his hand protectively on both their shoulders.

"It's fine," I assured her. "This time, I feel like I've been in a car accident."

Cane entered, followed by a brunette carrying a baby. Charlie ran straight over to them and dragged the woman and baby forward. "This is Aunt Thea," she said, taking it upon herself to introduce us. "And this is Uncle Cane and Aunt Thea's baby. My cousin," she added proudly.

"It's lovely to finally meet you," Thea said, and I nodded likewise while trying not to be jealous that the most stunning woman I had ever seen gave birth only a few days ago. She looked like she'd just stepped from the covers of a magazine while I 'looked like I'd been in a car accident.'

Rex and Lucky entered, carrying a huge teddy bear and what must be a dozen balloons between them.

"Have you decided on a name for the baby yet?" Lucky asked. "Or do we keep calling her the baby?"

"We've decided on Toni, if that's okay with you?" Cane said while looking at Bono.

Bono smiled. "Toni's perfect."

"It's not for you, Charlie-baby," Amber said when she noted the little girl's eyes hadn't left the teddy. "It's for Aunt Hope, to help her feel better."

I glanced at Bono. Aunt Hope. I liked the sound of that.

"That's okay," Charlie said and inched closer to me, smiling. "Daddy's getting me a puppy named Buttons."

I laughed. "Buttons is a fine name for a puppy."

The visit didn't last much longer. I grew tired and everyone gave me their best wishes and left, including Craig Weathers, who also popped in to make sure I was doing okay.

Only Bono remained. He grabbed his chair and pulled it right next to the bed and grasped both my hands and stared at them, never looking me in the eye. I knew he was beating himself up all over again.

I cupped his chin in my hands and turned his face toward me. "You've always been my hero. Did you know that? I hated my life and never thought I'd make it to twenty, let alone thirty-four. Hell, I never wanted to until I met you. Do you remember the first time we laid eyes on each other?"

"You winked at me," he said, and a cheeky grin played at his lips.

"Did you ever wonder why I winked at you?"

"Because you were always stronger than I was."

I shook my head and laughed. "Rubbish. I winked because you looked like you either wanted to kill me or kiss me. I winked as I thought it would be the quickest way to piss you off and find out which one it was." I brushed my hand over his lips. "When that same silly grin took over your face, I knew which one it was and that I'd found a reason to call a place home."

Bono leaned down and gently pressed his lips to my own. "And where will you call home now that you can be Hope Fisher?" he asked when he pulled back.

I shrugged. "I said goodbye to Hope Fisher a long time ago. But, if you'll have me, Hope Travers wouldn't be averse to settling in Colorado."

Bono shook his head. "Is that your idea of a proposal?" he asked and kissed me again.

"No. It's a reminder that you gave one to me."

Bono slipped the engagement ring from my right hand and onto my finger on my left. "I've never forgotten."

I smiled and bit my bottom lip. "Do you know what you have forgotten?" I said. Bono shook his head. "To get me food. I'm still starving." Bono laughed. "Pizza would be great," I added, and he kissed me again before pulling away.

"Fine," he said. "But no pineapple."

"Aww, but I'm injured and trapped in a hospital bed. Shouldn't your hero complex want to give in to my every whim?"

Bono rolled his eyes. "Fine, just this once, you can have pineapple," he said before looking at me intently. And when you're healed, then I'll give in to your every whim."

I pulled him back down for a final kiss before sending him to get me food. "Actually," I called as he was stepping through the door, "I'll think I'll give in to yours."

~

Printed in Great Britain
by Amazon